- IN THE GIANT'S SHADOW -

THE

FOREIGN DEEP

PETE A O'DONNELL

The Foreign Deep

Copyright ©2025 Pete A O'Donnell

Cover image by Miblart

First Printing, 2025

ISBN: 978-1-7349090-1-2

Ill-Advised Stories
PO Box 6072 Warwick, RI 02887
www.illadvisedstories.com

Also By

The Curse of Purgatory Cove

In the Giants Shadow
Book 1: The Stars Beyond the Mesa
Book 3The Voice of Stones
Book 4 The Calling of Ghosts

And for younger readers:
The Merlin's Visit the Fire Station

CHAPTER 1

Near the palace's heart, Jayse heard distant waves as his footsteps echoed off the hallway's vaulted ceilings. Below him, through arched openings, grand chambers and tropical gardens soaked in the light of distant suns, while in the azure sky, the silhouette of the star blossom, an elevator to space, was a black spot tied to the surface of the ocean world, Grannus. Jayse touched the closest banister, not feeling the heat cast off from the white masonry. The walls and ornate columns of the royal citadel were made from coral, grown and harvested on the seabed, and polished into building material. He took little comfort from living in luxury. His father-in-law made certain of that.

Voices came from further ahead, from the high chief's council chamber, in a suite of rooms set aside for the ruler and his family. Advisers laughed, a deep rolling sound of camaraderie. They slapped each other on their backs, satisfied with whatever had been decided inside. As Jayse appeared at the corner, the men glanced behind and stopped talking like he was the joke.

The old men were in their grandest clothing, bejeweled but showing their aged bodies. The climate of the capital city, Anchor Home, didn't allow for heavy apparel. Even formal wear had the look of beach clothing. It was all sashes and breechcloths, occasionally shortened trousers, showing the bellies and wrinkles of the nobles. Though he was young and fit, if a bit thin, Jayse didn't care for the fashion. He'd been a soldier once and a man from the north, where people were more modest.

His father-in-law wasn't in the hall with the others. The high chief was still inside his chamber. Jayse barely greeted the councilors as he pushed through, making his way to the heavy doors and going in. They were open just enough to allow a single person to pass.

It took a moment for his eyes to adjust. The council chamber was one of the few spaces in the palace that wasn't filled with natural light. A small skylight high above, and glowing lamps along the walls, gave the only illumination. It was a room meant to be sealed, to hold state secrets. That's why he was surprised to see a man from a foreign power inside, a royal envoy of the Tamerlane dynasty that ruled the world of Uppsala.

Most of the people on Grannus, Jayse included, showed an Asian ancestry, with epicanthal folds shaping their eyes. The man from Uppsala had Asian heritage as well, but his features were from the lands that once bordered Africa and Europe— the dark hair and pale brown skin of India. They were places lost to time, while the traits remained on worlds circling stars far from the Sol system.

Jayse's eyes went from the envoy to the high chief as he demanded, "My Liege, what is the meaning of this?" Immediately, he wished he hadn't blurted it out. He wanted to show that he was angry while still maintaining some degree of respect. In truth, he didn't want to do this at all, but he heard his wife's voice, telling him he'd taken too much, that her father had put him at arm's length long enough. Since the high chief took a new bride, her insistence had grown.

High Chief Augustine leaned over the massive table in the center of the room and the pile of reports stacked on it. "The meaning of what exactly?" His bushy eyebrows curled down as his eyes came alight.

"I'm sorry," Jayse stammered, lowering his head and bowing, giving the chief his due respect. He pointed to the man from Uppsala. "You invited a foreigner into council while I was left out. That's what I'd like an explanation for."

The envoy stood next to Ascari, the king's war leader. Years ago, when Jayse served his time in the Grannus defense force, Ascari had been a distant name, head of the entire military. It was strange to be in the same room with him. Jayse had been a chief's son then, but his father's domain in the north had meant little to anyone in Anchor Home. Jayse served among the commoners. 'If you were to lead, you had to serve your time,' his father always said. That was long before his marriage to the high chief's daughter, his only heir.

Pulling a sheet of paper from beneath his sash, Jayse dropped it on the table and said, "I read the intel report. Hundreds of ships are falling toward us, coming down the well from Uppsala. It's an armada."

The high chief stood to his full height, crossing his arms. Despite his years, he was still fit, reminding Jayse of the pilings on a dock, tall, stiff, and unbreakable. "Emperor Tamerlane has sent an envoy to allay our fears. To assure us that his fleet is not moving on Grannus," Augustine said.

The envoy put his hand out to Jayse. "I'm Lord Beleeze. We met at your wedding. Though I wouldn't be surprised if you don't remember me. That was a well-attended ceremony."

"And expensive," the high chief said with little humor.

Going to the table and picking the report up, Ascari said to Jayse, "You're missing the top page. The one marked secret. How did you get this?"

Jayse held his back stiff. "It doesn't matter. In a day, everyone will know. An amateur with a telescope will see their engine flares. While you're having your secret meetings, people will be in a panic."

The high chief ignored him and said to Ascari, "I'm sure it was my daughter. She keeps her ears open." The chief turned to the man from Uppsala. "Would you care to answer the prince?"

The envoy held his hands open. "Of course." He turned to Jayse. "My emperor means your world no harm. He is going to the ring, to the squatters there. Those pirates and scum have been allowed a lawless life for too long. I'm sure you've heard of them attacking our shipping. We've lost transports, as have you. Anyone who drops too close to Altor risks being raided. It can't be allowed to go on. We're trying to keep this expedition quiet to avoid warning them."

Both Uppsala and Grannus circled a massive gas giant called Altor. There were three other worlds: Tarnish, Einherjar, and Oighear. Uppsala was the crown jewel of all those moons, more capable of supporting human life than the others, making it the most formidable in the system. Grannus was better suited for people with gills as most of its surface was covered in water.

Jayse thought of the ring, the broken collection of rocks that circled above Altor, the very edge of human civilization. Grannus was not a world rich in metals. Over the years, they'd traded with the colonies there. When ships went missing, it was easy to blame the strange people whose bodies had been changed by low gravity in the ring, living in small clans alongside Long-Wolfs. Perhaps they were lawless, as the man from Uppsala said, but not all of them were criminals. Most were like any other people, wanting to live in peace.

Watching Ascari, Jayse tried to read his face, wondering if he believed this explanation. Recently, the military commander questioned the pirate attack's authenticity, warning that it could be aggression by the nobles of Uppsala. Ascari remained unreadable, staring back as he folded Jayse's paper and tucked it away.

Stepping past the envoy, Jayse closed in on the high chief. "An entire armada will pass in striking distance of our home, and you feel no urge to say anything to your people? If you want to take this man's word, fine, but we should still prepare our citizens, and we should warn the True Grannusians." Jayse's hands opened, pointing down.

A noise, possibly a laugh, escaped the Envoy, though it sounded cruel and was hidden by a quick throat clearing.

Jayse watched the high chief's lip pull up in a sneer at the term, 'True Grannusian,' before saying, "There is nothing for our neighbors to fear. Besides, they keep their secrets and see more than you know."

Jayse pointed to the envoy. "Even if they aren't coming here. This attack will weaken us. We trade with the people in the Belt. We build ships with their metal—"

"Enough!" the high chief shouted. "This has all been discussed. If I'd wanted your opinion, I would've called you here."

Jayse felt his face turn red. "Very well. I'm glad that I know now. I'm glad you've been clear on how you see me." He started toward the door, regretting how pouty he sounded.

The high chief ran his hand down either side of his mustache and called, "Wait!" in a tone that wasn't to be ignored. As Jayse came to a stop, the chief pointed to the exit and told Ascari and Beleeze, "Give us the room." He came around the table and followed them to the door. As they left, he closed it behind them and turned around to face his son-in-law.

Jayse had expected anger, but the high chief kept his voice low. "You think I'm foolish, don't you?"

"No, of course not," Jayse stammered as the man closed the distance between them. The room suddenly felt tight.

Reaching out and taking his shoulders, Augustine came in close. His hands were like iron on his arms. "Good, because I'm not. I don't suffer them either. You are my daughter's husband. I chose you, Jayse. I, and I alone, brought you from that cold hunk of ice you call home. Not because I needed another advisor, but because I needed an alliance with your father." He pushed Jayse back against the table, "If I decide to include you in a meeting, then by all means, show up. If I don't, stay the hell away, boy."

Jayse broke his grip and pushed his arms away, but he was off-balance with a chair behind his legs. The chief gave a single shove, just enough that he fell over, stumbling on the chairs.

Standing over him and looking down, the high chief scoffed. "All you've succeeded in doing today is making yourself look weak, and through you, my rule." He stepped back, wringing his hands, wiping them down his royal sash. "I know this wasn't your idea, that my daughter put you up to it, so I will forgive this transgression, but I warn you, do not test my patience again. I will be less forgiving next time." The

high chief left the room as Jayse pulled himself to his feet.

He grabbed the back of one of the seats and picked it up, ready to throw it, but all he did was squeeze the sides, looking at the exit and his father-in-law's back.

CHAPTER 2

An agonizing amount of time passed in the council chamber as Jayse waited, hoping the hallway would be empty when he left. He didn't want to see any of those fat councilors. The old men, he was sure, knew exactly what had happened between him and the high chief. In the world of politics, the experienced were worse than the young with their talk and gossip, enthralled by tales of weakness, always looking for someone to keep low. It was the only way to make certain that they didn't become the next whipping boy.

Jayse opened the door slowly, hating himself a bit as he did. He'd made his move, tried to assert himself after years of being ignored and ended up on the floor for it. The corridor was empty. Sneaking out like a thief, he made his way back to his own suite, where he knew his wife would be waiting to hear how it went.

Daoine had told him to stand up for himself, to call her father out. The high chief was covering up the movement of the Tamerlane fleet. She'd assured him it was a dire threat that couldn't be ignored. even going as far as to invoke the safety of their children, their two-year-old son, and the one that wasn't born yet. He had to do it for their future.

Jayse shook his head, imagining facing her, telling her what happened. His steps slowed. On a back staircase, he struggled to move his feet. He looked out at the vast ocean and wished he could sail away from this place, back to the north. He missed the simplicity of life before all this. He missed his days as a soldier, when the right thing to do was what his officer told him to.

Jayse slammed his hand against the banister and took a deep breath, continuing on his way. Passing guards, he entered their suite on the first floor and found the elegant rooms empty. Out the back was their corner of the garden. He heard voices. His son's was young and squeaky, filled with laughter. A man's voice was there as well. Jayse paused at the door, trying to imagine who it could be. It sounded familiar. When he recognized the timber and laughter of an old friend, a smile nearly broke out, but he shook it away, still thinking of the high chief and his embarrassment. His closest friend wasn't the welcome sight he should've been after all these months. Selfish as it was, Jayse would rather be alone.

Coming to the opening, he saw Cathal. He didn't wear his uniform but dressed in simple island clothing that did nothing to hide his muscular physique. His shorts and sash were disheveled as he ran, flying in figure eights with Jayse's son, Cormack, on his back. He circled the small grassy lawn with his elbows out wide, like wings, as he gripped the giggling boy's feet.

He was playing the part of a sea dragon as he told the boy a story. Squatting down, coming in for a landing, he said with vigor, "And then the dragons would race up from the bottom of the ocean! They'd go fast as lightning while their Naiad riders held on!" Cathal leapt into the air with Cormack still on his back, yelling, "Breaching the surface, they'd tear the ships apart, sending their hunters to the bottom!" The boy laughed, still holding on as the soldier came down, landing on all fours.

Princess Daoine sat on a bench in front of brightly colored flowers, watching her son as she explained, "Don't forget, the men hunting them were our ancestors. Yours and mine, Cathal. You make us sound dreadful."

With her pregnancy well underway, the princess glowed. Her belly had pushed out early with this second child. Sitting or standing, she constantly touched its round surface. It'd be another season before the child was born, but already, she'd felt it kicking.

As stern as Daoine's father's features were, the same angles made for a refined beauty in his daughter, softened with the life growing in her. Jayse knew that in anger, she could still turn back to sharpness, darkening with an imperialist edge. Seeing her demure smile, watching Cathal, Jayse wondered how fast it would vanish when he told her how the meeting had gone.

Cathal said to the princess, "Yes, we were victors. We wrote the history, but reading between the lines, I'm not sure we come off so well."

Daoine shook her head and turned her eyes to Jayse as he hid a sour expression behind a forced smile. He said, "Not every noble house hunted the Naiads. Some defended them. Some were their allies."

"Did our family?" Cormack asked, still mounted on Cathal.

"Not mine." Jayse pointed to his chest. "Northerners stayed out of it altogether, like we do with most things."

"And Mommy's?" Cormack asked, pointing at her.

She laughed. "We're Sidhe. At one time or another, we fought everyone," she said, lunging forward and grabbing the child.

"Careful," Jayse said, watching his wife sweep the laughing boy up in her arms.

Cathal collapsed into the grass. "He's getting heavy. I think he broke my back."

Jayse came over and gave his friend a kick in the behind while the princess put her son back on the ground. The boy ran to Cathal with genuine concern on his face. "Don't kick him, Daddy."

Cathal rolled over onto his back, snatching Cormack into the air, holding him with his feet dangling. "You could never break me, young prince. I'm made of iron and steel." He let Cormack go as Jayse offered him a hand up from the ground. Cathal was much shorter. He barely reached Jayse's chin, but his neck was thick, and his shoulders were wide, and the muscles of his arms flexed with every movement.

"What brings you here?" Jayse asked, still holding his friend's hand as he gave him a hug. They hadn't seen each other in months as Cathal had been away, assigned to sub duty. While Jayse had stepped away from the military, Cathal had gone on, joining a special unit of divers, an all-purpose response team.

"I'm on leave for a few days. Not enough time to go home, so I thought I'd see how things are here. See if my friend had any interest in draining a pint or two in town." Cathal turned to the queen and gave an elaborate bow. "My lady, can Jayse come out and play?"

Daoine rolled her eyes. "Maybe, but first, may I have a moment to speak to him in private?"

Cathal looked between the two and knew it was something serious. "Yes, of course. Cormack, why don't you show me your room?" Cathal pointed back into the suite.

As he stepped away, Daoine turned to her husband and asked in a low voice. "I take it from the look on your face it didn't go well?"

Jayse held up his hands. "Your father didn't want me there and nothing I did changed his mind. He believes that Tamerlane is only going to attack the clans in the belt."

She put her hand on his chest. "Were you forceful? He respects strength."

"I was, I was—"

She closed her fist and tapped him lightly, looking up into his eyes. "Jayse, he's playing a dangerous game. He needs to defend our world. My father doesn't know Tamerlane like we do. You remember how he was on Nalanda; even the monks were scared of him." For the past hundred years, all the young nobles and rulers from the different worlds were educated at a school in the belt. An ancient space station, it was built by inhuman hands and staffed by an order of monks, serving violent gods.

When they were there, Tamerlane was a driven upperclassman of particular intelligence and ability. Tamerlane's influence over the head monk and the other students seemed natural. He was never outwardly cruel or demanding. In fact, his natural charisma made him an easy person to like.

Still, everyone was careful around him. It wasn't out of fear of falling in the social order, but for darker reasons. Whispers and rumors of grim happenings surrounded Tamerlane, stories of rivals disappearing. Jayse shook his head, recalling those days. "Of course I remember. There was an envoy with your father in the meeting. He was from Uppsala, and you know as well as I that there's been talk of—"

Daoine interrupted him for the second time. "No, he would never."

Jayse reached out and touched her shoulders, finishing his sentence. "Give fealty to Tamerlane. Avoid a war altogether with appeasement. I think he might."

She pushed him away, shaking her head. "He doesn't have enough support for that. It would divide our world. We'd be at war with each other instead."

Jayse shrugged. "But one side, your father's, would have the backing of Tamerlane's armada. He would have peace through dominance. The same way Tamerlane took the kingdoms of Uppsala."

"And our world would belong to a foreign ruler." Daoine looked disgusted. She touched her pregnant belly and huffed as she paced.

"What are you thinking?" Jayse asked.

"It's better you don't know." She bit the words off, staring at the ground and turning her head slightly, thinking. She patted his chest and brought her eyes back up to meet his again. "Go with your friend. Catch up. But keep the rest of this to yourself. You did what you could. It'll be my turn next."

She was about to walk away from him when she added. "Oh, by the way, the doctor said he had some news for us." Her hand moved against her belly. "We've got an appointment with him late this afternoon. Please go easy with Cathal. I'm not sure what it's about, and I need you standing upright when we get there." She smiled, but it was a timid thing.

Jayse watched her eyes go down; her attention was on the life growing in her. He touched her arm. "I promise, I'll only be gone a few hours," Jayse said.

CHAPTER 3

The two friends started at a small tavern near one of the hundreds of jetties that lined Anchor Home's western shore. It was a place for sailors with small tables crowded together, but the fish stew was fresh, and the seaweed wraps were salty. No one recognized Jayse, or they were too polite to call him out, but the bartender greeted Cathal by name. Laughing, Cathal shook the man's hand and asked after his family. He spent more time with him than one would expect, leaving his friend, Prince Jayse, waiting. When he finally sat, he held up two fingers for drinks.

The beer was strong, and when they were done eating, the man gave them a bucketful on ice and loaned them a few fishing poles to take down to the rocky jetty. Carefully, they made their way out along the stones, passing other men fishing.

They whiled away midday and the afternoon, casting and catching very little, laughing as they slowly got drunk and talked about their days serving together. Other than telling his friend it hadn't gone well, Jayse was careful not to give any details of the morning meeting away. He could trust Cathal, but it was still privileged information, not meant to be shared.

Everyone would know about Tamerlane's fleet in a few days anyway. There was no way to hide the movement of so many ships. It'd be on public feeds and visible in the sky. Occasionally, Jayse looked overhead, past the dark spot of the star blossom. He wondered what it'd be like to see so many ships. Would their drive trails be visible in the daylight, scorching across the sky?

Cathal told Jayse about his recent missions. Mostly, they were small rescue operations, but he knew his friend had done more. In a decade of service, he'd fought terrorists and aided local lords to put down insurrections, following orders he may not have believed in.

They were three beers in, when Cathal said to Jayse, "I lied to you earlier."

"About what?" Jayse asked. They sat with their feet dangling above the water, their poles held loose in their hands.

"I'm not on leave. Officially, I'm retired." Cathal tilted his head. "Or maybe the term is fired."

"What happened?" Jayse glanced at his friend, who kept his eyes forward on the water.

Cathal sighed, never turning his head. "I was given a better offer. To be honest, I was tired of the work. You know, the dirty work. It was never for me. I said no too many times, and they told me to pack my things."

Jayse waited for him to say more, to tell him the whole story, but Cathal stayed quiet, and he wouldn't push. "At least I'll have you around a little more."

"Sometimes," his friend said.

"What do you mean?"

"I'll tell you later." Cathal shrugged as his line ran out with a fish on.

The day passed, and the retired soldier managed to avoid discussing his future. Eventually, they started back to the little tavern, returning the bucket and poles before going their separate ways. As Jayse approached the palace, more and more people realized who he was, waving as he passed. He stopped at the main checkpoint where the guards looked at him strangely for wandering off the grounds alone.

Daoine greeted him in the corridor. "Feeling better?" she asked, noticing the dopey smile on his face.

Jayse leaned in to kiss her, saying, "Much better."

She scoffed, turning away and pinching her nose at the smell of yeast on his breath. "Are you going to be able to listen to the doctor?"

Jayse held his hands up to his ears. "What? Speak up," he asked comically. Occasionally, the princess would laugh at one of his jokes. Their marriage had been arranged, sealing the bond between two clans. They got along better than most would have expected, forming a friendship that had little to do with physical intimacy. Slowly over the years, especially after Cormack was born, it turned into something like love.

The princess shook her head, turning and starting off. "When this baby is out of me, I'm going to make you pay. It'll be my turn to have a few in the afternoon while you watch the children."

He chased after her. "I didn't have that much. We mostly fished."

She turned and looked him up and down, noticing his empty hands. "Not very well."

"I swear I caught some real monsters." He held his hands wide. "Cathal made me throw them back. He's very particular about only keeping what we'd eat."

"I'm sure," Daoine said.

"Did you want me to clean them and serve them to you? I do know how to do that." With a silly smile, he pointed his thumb at his chest.

"That's exactly what I wanted," She snapped and shook her head, all the playfulness gone as she walked on. "Let's just get this over with."

Too busy trying to forget this morning, Jayse hadn't been thinking about what this appointment might mean to his wife, that when a doctor said he had news to tell both parents, a mother-to-be would be worried. He suddenly felt awful, realizing how she'd kept her thoughts and fears to herself.

He took her arm and, in a far more sober tone, said, "I'm sorry. Really, we didn't have that much. I promise, I'm good. Let's go find out what this is about, okay?" He pulled her back and hugged her. She leaned in for a quick moment. Daoine wasn't one for displays of emotion. This quick embrace was as close as she got to admitting she was scared.

Hand in hand, they made their way to the palace's medical clinic. It was on the first floor in one of the oldest and most secure parts of the building. The structure was half-buried, with walls of concrete and reinforced steel. Not elegant like the rest of the palace, it had stood through wars and bombardment. It still showed signs of being outfitted for past armies, with too many beds and too much space for the common work it did now. Jayse and Daoine passed a façade of white and entered the passage of rougher walls. The fading afternoon light shone down through windows on the far side of a long hall filled with empty beds. They went to the desk below those windows.

The woman there stood up as they approached. She stepped out so that she could bow more deeply. Daoine took the gesture with grace, while it made Jayse uncomfortable. People didn't bow to the nobility in the north, not like this.

"We're here to see Doctor Kimura," Princess Daoine said, glancing at an opening behind the woman, noticing that the lights were off.

"I'm very sorry, Your Majesty. Doctor Kimura hasn't reported to work today. He was gone early, bringing vaccines to the farmers on the moored islands. He must've been delayed. He was supposed to be back hours ago." The woman moved her hands, wringing them as she kept her eyes low.

The princess touched her belly again. "He asked me to meet here now. It sounded important."

"I'm very sorry. I will wait here for him, and as soon as he comes in, I'll send him to you," the woman promised.

Jayse looked at the fading light. It was near the end of the day, when secretaries and domestic workers left the palace, returning to their apartments in Anchor Home. Only the guards, barracked soldiers, and kitchen staff stayed on. He was tempted to tell the woman to go home, but looking at his wife, he knew she expected her to do as she said, even if it meant staying late into the night.

"Thank you." Daoine nodded and left.

Jayse had to hurry to catch up to her. "Are you okay?" he asked.

She bit her lip. "I don't care for things being unresolved." She pointed back to the room. "But I suppose it can't be that important if the man didn't bother to show up. Perhaps it's time the palace found a more reliable doctor."

Jayse didn't say anything, choosing not to disagree with his wife. They made their way back to their suite, where Cormack waited with a nanny. Most nights, they were expected to dine in the high chief's hall, but they sent word that they wouldn't be joining the royal court. They had food brought to them. "If he has a problem with it, he can come tell me," Daoine said as they sat and had a meal as a family.

Jayse didn't believe that even the high chief would choose such a foolish battle with his wife.

CHAPTER 4

Near the palace but far enough away not to sully its stately beauty was a naval base. Warships and skimmers lined the docks, and weapons emplacements with anti-aircraft guns and rockets stood vigilant, but this was only what could be seen on the surface. Down below the water line, reaching even under the palace, was a larger military installation, where a fleet of submarines surfaced into hangar bays and launch tubes. There were barracks, commissaries, and storage for long sieges. In times of war, the installation would be crowded with men and women, bound for combat, but in this time of relative peace, only a skeleton crew remained.

Late at night, lonely guards patrolled the dimly lit passages made for the small attack subs, the backbone of deep-sea warfare. In one of these bays that looked like a flooded subway tunnel, a sub slowly crept to the surface with all of its running lights extinguished. It was painted a blackish green and had no windows, no weak spots in its hull. The guard, who should've been alerting the entire base to this unscheduled arrival, stood back and watched as the vessel pushed up to the dock.

Its top hatch opened, and four men climbed out, the last two carrying a heavy load that they dumped roughly onto the dock. They were unconcerned as someone inside the lumpy bag groaned in pain. The men were dressed in dark clothing with tactical helmets, hiding their faces and receiving intel through their heads-up displays.

The men stood around the bag. "Open it," their officer ordered, a man by the name of Skellis. Two others went to work, untying the sack. Dark eyes, too large for a human's face, were revealed. This creature looked up at them with fear. It was something like a man. He had light-grey skin, and his hair was black and long. He wore a simple suit that was slick and tight around his torso but with spaces left open along his sides for flaps in his grey skin. His hands and legs were tied, and his mouth was gagged.

"I've never seen one before," the guard said, keeping his distance.

"Few have. These monsters are sneaky," Skellis said. He waved his hand toward the ceiling as he

ordered his men, "Stand him up."

Two reached down to the Naiad, took him by each arm, and faced him toward the sub. "Should we cut him loose?" one asked. The Naiad struggled. With his feet bound, he couldn't move very well, but he shoved with his elbows.

"I wouldn't; they're stronger than us," Skellis said. He walked over to the guard and handed him a long cylinder. "Put this on your side arm."

The guard pulled his pistol from its holster and screwed the silencer on.

"You know what to do." Skellis motioned to the Naiad, who was still facing away, though he twisted his head to see what would happen to him.

The guard pointed his weapon at the prisoner's back. He hesitated, staring down the long barrel. Gritting his teeth, he finally pulled the trigger. There were two short, angry noises and the sound of bullets hitting flesh.

The Naiad stopped struggling and went limp, hanging down between the two men. They dropped him to the ground. One stood back, wiping his hands in disgust, while the other took out a long knife with a detailed handle. He cut the bindings from the dead Naiad's hands and removed the gag.

"All right, let's move. We're on a clock now," Skellis said. He pointed at the silencer. "Throw that back in the sub." Then he tapped the guard on the shoulder. "And make sure our path is clear when we return. Anyone who gets in the way becomes a casualty. No witnesses."

The guard nodded, and the four men started off. They followed a map to an access tunnel. Working through half-forgotten passages, they made their way up through the subbase. They found a drainage tunnel that crossed into the palace grounds, running down to a grated cover. When they knocked it clear and climbed up, they were in the garden, not far from where Cathal had played with Cormack earlier that day. It was a short distance to the back door of Jayse and Daoine's suite.

CHAPTER 5

There was a noise in the middle of the night. Jayse opened his eyes. His two-year-old son was breathing noisily next to him, his mouth hanging open. The lamp by the bed glowed softly. Jayse had fallen asleep in Cormack's bed, reading to the boy. Jayse's eyes searched over the room, wondering what woke him.

Daoine was at the point in her pregnancy where she couldn't get comfortable, so most nights, over the past month, Jayse either passed out in here, or he'd go to the sofa in their den. The beer in the afternoon had worn off by story time. Sleep hadn't been far behind.

Jayse looked at the door. He assumed it was Daoine moving about. He snuck out of Cormack's bed, trying not to disturb him. Looking back, his heart was nearly overwhelmed by his son's peaceful face. Cormack could've carried him halfway across the palace, and the boy would've slept on. Jayse envied him for that weightlessness, that freedom from the worries and thoughts that pulled on him.

Tiptoeing to the door, Jayse stepped out and closed it softly behind him, noticing that the rest of their suite was still dark. If Daoine was up, he would've expected her to turn on a light or to at least see the glow from their icebox. She often went to their small kitchen to find a late-night snack.

He thought of calling for her. For some reason, he hesitated, trying to ignore the feeling that something wasn't right. The silence in the hallway felt heavy as the hairs on the back of his neck stood up. He walked quietly toward the kitchen, telling himself he was being silly, expecting any moment to see his wife in the pantry.

He came around the corner and found the kitchen empty. There was no sign that she'd even been there. He thought of turning on a light himself. Instead, he went on, past the den and toward his bedroom. They had a private washroom inside. He assumed that was where he would find Daoine.

Looking down the dark hall, he noticed the door half open to their bedroom and the lights off inside. If his wife was asleep, if there was nothing amiss, then the last thing he wanted to do was bother her. For a moment, he thought of ignoring the growing pit in his stomach and going to the den to lie back down, but something told him to check on her. As he reached for the handle, he heard a strange noise inside, a quick escape of air. As he asked himself what it could be, there was something far clearer, the low whispering of voices.

Adrenalin spiked through Jayse as he shoved the door open and burst in. A window across the room allowed the soft glow from the night sky and the garden lights to shine down on his marriage bed where his wife's form lay still.

Surrounding her were three dark figures. One was bent down over Daoine. He scooped her up in his arms.

The three men turned at his entrance. None spoke as they stared through their tactical helmets.

"Get away from her!" Jayse yelled, charging the closest one.

The man took a step back. His facemask was open, revealing his mouth. He held a long cylinder to it. There was that sound again, the sudden escape of air. A sharp sting brought Jayse's attention to his chest, where a dark barb stuck out.

As he touched it, someone said, "Hit him again," and the sound came once more. This time, his neck was pierced. Jayse's legs became weak. His arms felt heavy. He leaned against the door frame and for a moment, he didn't understand why the men were getting taller, not until he felt the floor. He was already in darkness by the time his whole body fell back, slumping over unconscious.

CHAPTER 6

Bed after bed, in rows, surrounded Jayse when his eyes opened. At the far end of a long room, sunlight poured in. His eyes met the nurse's behind her desk, and he knew he was in the medical clinic, though he had no idea how he'd gotten here. She picked up a hand terminal and spoke, "He's awake."

"What happened?" Jayse tried to ask, but his mouth was so dry, it came out as a croak. She offered him a glass of water. Lifting his hand, he reached for it and missed, unsure why. His limbs felt like they were made of lead. "Go easy," she said, helping him sit up and bring the glass forward again. Opening his mouth, he pulled in a long swig as he heard footsteps.

Cathal had been sitting across the room. He put a hand on Jayse's shoulder as he tried to sit up. "Hey there, slim. You've been out for a while. Go easy."

"How did I get here?" Jayse asked, feeling woozy.

Cathal opened his mouth to answer, but as he did, he turned his eyes back to the nurse's desk and the doctor's private office. A woman came out that Jayse had never seen before. "Who's that?" he asked.

"The new doctor," Cathal said.

The middle-aged woman, with her greying hair tied up in a bun, stepped beside him. "My prince, you've been out for a while. I'd like to check a few things," the doctor said, going past the nurse. A screen next to the bed made Jayse realize a number of wires were attached to him.

He reached out, grabbing Cathal's arm, his coordination already improving. "I don't understand. Where are Cormack and Daoine?"

Cathal touched his friend's shoulder. "Cormack is with your nanny. I spent most of the morning with him. He's doing okay. And Daoine—" He stopped, looking up again. More footsteps approached.

"That's the important question, isn't it?" Commander Ascari, the head of Grannus's defense force, approached.

Cathal dropped his voice. "You were attacked. Like the doc said, you've been out for a while."

"Captain," Ascari said, nodding to acknowledge Cathal. The defense force was too big for Ascari to know every rank-and-file officer, but Cathal's team had performed enough special operations that he'd seen his name plenty of times. Being the prince's closest friend wasn't the type of thing Ascari would fail to notice either.

The man wasn't much taller than Cathal, with a similar build, though he wasn't quite as muscular. In every other way, he was Cathal's opposite, never smiling, permeating the air with a sense of disapproval. His age was hard to guess because his hair was jet black, and his face was tight. His cheekbones bulged below deep-set dark eyes. "Doctor, can you give us a moment?" he asked.

The woman nodded and backed away without question, taking the nurse with her. They both went into the private office and closed the door. This was Ascari's effect. Everyone knew to be scared of him.

Jayse became more alert and annoyed that no one had given him an answer yet. "Where is my wife?" he demanded.

Ascari did his best version of concern, sighing and lowering his head. It fell shy of sincerity. "She was kidnapped. Taken out of your suite over a day ago."

"What?" Jayse sat up quickly and became dizzy.

"Easy, easy." Cathal took his shoulder again. "You've been out for a day and a half."

"How?" Jayse asked.

"You were poisoned." Ascari took a small bag out of his pocket and hung it in Jayse's face. Inside was a dart with hardened bone-like ridges. "Have either of you ever seen one of these before?"

Jayse shook his head while Cathal took the bag, looking closely at it. His face was unreadable as he handed it back.

"Well," Ascari demanded.

Cathal nodded. "It's a dart from a blow gun. Some southern tribes like mine will use them in hunting birds and such."

Raising an eyebrow, Ascari corrected him, "You know that's not what this is. Note the spurs on the back. This was made to be fired underwater."

Cathal admitted, "The Naiads once used darts like these."

Ascari showed his teeth in a gesture that fell shy of being a smile. "You mean they 'use' such weapons."

Cathal tilted his head, unsure what the man meant.

Ascari put the bag away and explained, "We found a dead Naiad near the attack sub tubes. A guard managed to get a few shots off before they killed him. We found one of their knives buried in his chest."

Jayse looked at Cathal, trying to read anything from his friend's face. What Ascari said all sounded impossible. Naiads hadn't been seen in close to a century. They'd always lived separate from the rest of Grannus. After the arrival of the Aesir and their ban on genetic manipulation, the nobles of this world went out of their way to wipe them out, to cleanse them. It was a quick and dirty war, as the Naiad population was already small. Their cities were crushed, and their people were hunted to extinction. There were rumors that some still lived, that they had hidden homes in deeper waters, but Jayse always thought those were just stories.

"What would they want with my wife?" Jayse asked.

"I was hoping you could shine some light on that. Tell me what happened, what you saw," Ascari asked.

Jayse recited all that he could remember, the little that there was. Then, Ascari asked him several questions, most of which he had no answer for. Ascari said at the end, "I'm sure the princess is still alive. The only reason they'd take her is for leverage. She's a hostage. Before long, they will make their demands clear. Already, the high chief has sent out dozens of ships to scour the ocean floor. He'll be calling up more in the days to come. He wants me to activate our whole navy in this pursuit." He looked at Cathal, who didn't bother to point out that he was retired.

Jayse looked around the clinic. "Where is the high chief now?"

"He's calling in resources from other tribes," Ascari said. He cleared his throat. "He'll be greeting them out on the west jetty this afternoon. For now, get some rest. This is all well in hand."

Ascari bowed slightly, then turned to Cathal. "Captain, may I have a word with you?" he said, walking away without looking to see if Cathal followed him. They stopped by the door and spoke briefly. Cathal nodded, agreeing to something before he turned back to Jayse.

Jayse watched Ascari go, and as his friend returned, he asked, "What was that about?"

"Nothing, he just wants me to keep an eye on you." Cathal looked at the ceiling as he spoke, adding, "None of this makes sense."

"What do you mean?" Jayse asked.

Cathal held his hands high. "Naiads want nothing to do with us."

"How do you know?" Jayse noticed Cathal looking away again, not wanting to make eye contact.

His fingers touched his chin as he took a deep breath. "There are things I haven't told you. You need to know my only goal is to serve our world. It's what I've always tried to do." He paused while Jayse nodded with impatience. "I have friends with the True Grannusians."

Jayse pushed himself further up in the bed. He was tempted to swing his legs over the side. "Yes, I know a few too."

Cathal shook his head. "I'm not talking about their ambassadors or your teachers at Nalanda. I've been to their cities. They welcomed me into Twilight."

Pulling his knees up to his chest, Jayse said, "That's a rare honor, but it's not unheard of."

Cathal finally looked at him. "I've met the Naiads as well, there in the city."

Without moving or reacting, Jayse felt his chest tighten as he listened to Cathal's voice rise with excitement, "You should've seen it. They rode in on massive sea dragons, just like in the old stories. Eir wanted me to meet them. She knew I'd open my eyes and listen, and that perhaps..." He held his hands open. "Perhaps, when you and Daoine ruled, things could change. Things could be better for them."

Jayse felt his face flush. "When was this?"

"A few weeks ago."

"Then they showed up here?" Jayse snapped off. "First, they go to you, wanting you to influence me and my wife. Then they take her!" He sat forward, getting closer to Cathal. "Did you bring them here?"

Cathal stepped back, shaking his head. "No. That's not what they wanted."

"Then what?" Jayse demanded.

Cathal held up his hands. "They want a voice. They want to live in peace and not be hunted."

Jayse's brows dropped tight over his eyes, and he was closing his fists, ready to release his anger. Before he could, Cathal continued, "Did you know that? They're hunted for sport. They are people! Nobles think of them as prizes to be mounted on their walls. I've seen it with my own eyes. I've seen it, Jayse. They're not monsters. I'm telling you they're people, no different from us."

Jayse had so many thoughts. His anger was nearly choking him. He pointed his finger at Cathal. "I don't care what they are. They have my wife. You're going to help me get her back."

"Of course. Jayse, I'm your friend." Cathal tried reaching out to him.

"Stop it!" Jayse yelled, pulling his arm away. His heart pounded as he lowered his voice. "Friends don't come with secret agendas."

"Jayse—" Cathal started.

"No! I don't want to hear it. If you have friends with the True Grannusians, then use them like you intended to use me. Get them here, get me a meeting with these Naiads." Jayse swung his legs over the side.

"I will do all that I can," Cathal promised. "Where are you going?" he asked, watching his friend get to his feet. Jayse was wobbly, but when Cathal leaned in to help him, he raised his hand, telling him to back off.

"I'm going to get dressed, then I'm going to see my son," Jayse said. "After that, I'm going to the high chief. I expect you to have answers for me by then." He pointed toward the door.

Cathal backed away, holding his hands in the air.

CHAPTER 7

The doctor and nurse hadn't returned, and Jayse had just enough rage twisting inside him to try to leave soon after Cathal. He got surprisingly far before falling near the door. The clinic staff hurried as he caught himself, scooting to the wall. "Your Majesty, you need rest." The doctor bent down next to him.

"I need to see my son, and please don't call me that," Jayse grumbled as they helped him to his feet.

The two women looked at each other as Jayse softened his tone. "It's fine. I'm sorry. Call me whatever you need to. Just help me back to my quarters. Please. I want to see my son." He got his legs under him and started walking again with the nurse on one side and the doctor on the other.

Guards waited by his suite's door, and the nanny and a maid met them as it opened. They showed him to his sitting room, where Cormack was playing on the floor. Jayse felt his heart lift as he smiled at his son. The toxins in his system were working their way out, but he was still exhausted. Despite his protests that he was fine, the doctor stayed, monitoring for a while and giving him a concoction to take every few hours.

"Where's Momma?" Cormack asked as he climbed onto his father's lap.

"I'm not sure, but I'm going to find her," he promised.

Jayse drifted off with his son. He woke to the sound of gunfire. The distant boom of hunting rifles echoed through his window.

"I've got to go, Cormack," he said, waking the boy. The nanny came in and helped. It took a moment to steady his feet, but by the time Jayse reached the hallway, he was feeling better. A low simmer of rage carried him along, knowing that sound, aware of his father-in-law's habits.

Making his way through the palace, he wondered about his friend. Cathal met with the Naiads only weeks ago, then they showed up here. 'Did he betray them? Or perhaps let slip some detail that made them think they could get away with something like this?' Jayse shook his head. Cathal was smarter than that. He wasn't only a soldier but a specialist, trained to handle sensitive problems, the kind that every government ran into from time to time.

Reaching the northern gate, the sea gate, he passed soldiers, more than were usually here. Covering his eyes against the brightness of the twin suns, he looked around and saw warriors in armor, some bearing the insignia of the Sidhe and some wearing other clan's. There was a long jetty, part of a walled harbor, where the military skimmers waited in mooring fields and at docks.

In the distance, he saw the anchored islands like a string of green pearls rolling with the waves, looking like blossoming heads of broccoli. There were homes out there and farms as well, breaking through the walls of green. They weren't true islands, but floating barges built in the shells of massive sea creatures from the deepest parts of the ocean. Luckily, the kilometer-long leviathans floated when they died, giving the people of Grannus a chance to build. True islands, like Anchor Home, were few and far between.

In the sky, other creatures circled. The feathered kestrels had wing spans four meters wide and claws as long as a man's forearm. They plunged into the sea, disappearing for several minutes, then burst from the water with fish held in their talons, but their catch wasn't for them.

Water fell like rain from their wings as they climbed into the sky. From high above, they'd drop the fish, and the nobles posted on the jetty would take turns firing their rifles as they fell. It was the kind of game only the elite could enjoy because, first, it required trained Kestrels, and second, a hunter who'd never suffered hunger and was willing to waste so much meat. Jayse saw his father-in-law with a rifle to his shoulder. He fired, destroying an animal. The men around him patted him on his back, and he allowed a small smile to crack his face.

Jayse didn't care for the cruelty of the game, the wastefulness of it. Making his way out onto the rocky path, he thought of Cathal's words, that some nobles hunted Naiads, kept them for trophies. The story seemed more believable watching this indulgent display.

A good distance off, the men gathered around the high chief noticed him. They leaned in, whispering as Augustine rolled his eyes and opened the breach on his rifle, pulling the spent shells out and throwing them on the ground. "If you intend to join us, you'll need one of these," he called, holding the weapon up.

"I've no interest in playing games," Jayse said, watching his father-in-law reload and put the rifle to his shoulder. The game master held a whistle to his mouth, and one of the kestrels dropped from the sky, plunging into the water.

"It seems like an odd time for sport," Jayse called, coming to within a few meters of the high chief.

Augustine never turned his eyes. "In times of stress, it's important to find ways to relax." The kestrel shot back out of the water with a meter-long fish under it. Climbing high into the sky, it released the animal, and after a brief count, the chief pulled the trigger, blowing the fish's head clean off. The dismembered body dropped into water boiling with predators, waiting for a free meal.

"That's what this is? Your way of relieving stress?" Jayse didn't hide the disdain in his voice.

Augustine handed the rifle to a servant and said to the gathered men, "Excuse me," then he took Jayse's arm and walked him back, just out of earshot. "No, what this is, is politics. These men are lords and chiefs. Your own father is on his way and will be joining me tomorrow. Each of these men are here to pledge their support in the search for your wife." He pointed to the sky. "You're so worried about a foreign power from Uppsala. You forget that there are others right under the surface of our ocean." He motioned to the waves.

Jayse crossed his arms. "Gathering armies to pursue the Naiads makes no sense. There are so few, we thought they were extinct. Surely, you have enough vessels to search for them."

The chief leaned in. "You're not seeing the whole picture. Ask yourself why, why would they do this?

"Leverage," Jayse said.

"Yes, but for what? Think about their creators?"

Jayse's eyes went wide. "The True Grannusians have never been aggressive. Never like this. Why would you think they'd have anything to do with my wife's kidnapping?"

The high chief laughed and took a few steps back. "Northerners! Your heads are frozen. You are your father's oldest son; that's why you were given my daughter's hand. I wonder if any of your brothers would've been wiser." He paused, looking at Jayse, then shook his head, his eyes full of pity.

He stomped on the ground. "Do you know why I wanted an alliance with your people?"

Jayse tried to steady his voice. "Of course, the volcanism project." Jayse's tribe may not have wielded much political power, but they managed to survive in the harshest part of this world with a level of ingenuity rarely encountered. It all started with harnessing power, drilling deep wells into the ocean floor to extract heat, but then they conceived the idea of creating islands. It took generations to refine the technology and develop drills that could withstand the work without breaking down.

Augustine put his hands on his hips. "Yes, the volcanism project. You people thawed out long enough to come up with a good idea and your blood is pure."

"What does that have to do with my wife?"

The high chief jutted out his jaw. "The damn fish-heads don't want us making islands. What did they say? 'We should adapt to the world, not adapt the world to us.' That's what their ambassador said." He pointed to the sky and the massive shadow of the star blossom. "What the hell is that then? They build something that massive, but we try to change anything down there in the ocean, and it's some sort of assault on their world. We need land, and they want us to breathe water. It's time we assert our will. It's time we make clear this world is ours."

"So, what? They took Daoine as a hostage to stop us? Is that your theory?" Jayse asked, dumbfounded. He couldn't believe what he was hearing, what he thought the high chief was suggesting. He was talking about war with the True Grannusians.

"We'll find out soon enough. I'm marshaling forces." Augustine leaned in. "None of the clans will stand against me, against a father looking for his daughter." He stepped so close that Jayse was forced back.

"Of course not, but—"

The high chief grabbed his shoulders. "But what? Are you with us or against us?"

Jayse stepped back and said firmly, "I want my wife back. Whatever it takes."

Augustine ran his hand down his mustache and gave a brief nod while appraising his son-in-law. "Good. Make certain you tell your father that tomorrow. Make sure he knows to follow my lead."

Jayse wanted to say no. Wanted to call the man mad. But he nodded instead, saying, "I'm going back to my son now."

"Very well." Augustine turned around.

Picturing a war with the True Grannusians made Jayse want to escape, to run away from Anchor Home, go to his father and tell him not to come here. To stop what was coming before it could start. But he held his wits together. A thought scratched at the back of his head. Keeping his voice neutral, he asked, "Before I go, I was wondering why the palace doctor was replaced."

Augustine cleared his throat. "Because the other one is dead. They found his body out by the Anchor Islands. Apparently, he slipped while tending to some of the farmers. It was at night, so no one saw him go in."

"That's very sad," Jayse said, backing away. He felt his father-in-law's eyes on his back. He felt all of their eyes.

CHAPTER 8

The lights were brighter in Jayse's suite that night. He read to Cormack at bedtime and tried to reassure his son that everything would be okay, despite the fear that left his hands shaking and his mind reeling as he recalled what the high chief had said. The man was going to use his wife's kidnapping as leverage, a means to unite all the clans of Grannus, to assert their will over the True Grannusians. It was madness, angering the species that had allowed humans to live on this world for centuries, enabling them to prosper and grow.

He only managed to fall asleep after a long time and some strong medication. It was near dawn and for the second time in far too few nights, his eyes opened to a noise in the dark. "Don't call out. It's me," a voice said from the shadows. Cathal stepped toward his bed. He was dressed in dark clothing.

Jayse knew his suite was under watch, with guards at every entrance. "How did you get in here?" he asked, looking to the other side of the bed where Cormack was curled up in a ball, still deep asleep.

Cathal looked at the boy and smiled. "Sneaking into places is my specialty. Come on. We have an appointment."

Jayse stared at his friend until Cathal added, "You're the one who wanted to speak to the True Grannusians. Get dressed. Then meet me at the lagoon pool. Try not to let anyone follow you." He threw him some clothing, then disappeared into the hall.

Jayse pulled on his shorts and started after his friend but by the time he left the bedroom, Cathal was gone. The nanny came out into the hallway, slumber clouding her eyes. She asked him if something was the matter. "No," Jayse said. "I'm just having trouble sleeping. I thought I'd take a little walk to clear my head."

"Oh." She looked at him strangely.

Before leaving, he went back into his room and gave his son a kiss on the forehead. "I shouldn't be long," he said to the nanny as he left, going past his guards. "Keep an eye on them." He pointed back at the door, still wondering how Cathal had gotten in.

The lagoon was at the far end of the garden. He could've passed through the winding paths and tropical plants, but the hallway was a straighter route. He stepped out into a pillared courtyard that descended into a pool of calm water. There was an arch with a portcullis lowered, blocking the way. Beyond it, he saw the endless ocean, the reflection of the stars, and the early glow of dawn on the horizon.

Cathal waited at the water's edge with a large bundle. "Our guest just arrived." He pointed to the lagoon as Jayse stepped up to him. There were ripples on the surface and a dark mass moving below, coming closer. An alien head broke from the water, its large, glassy eyes shining in the pale light. It was shaped like a moray eel, slick from the water. A number of creatures dangled from its long, sinuous body. Below was a school of hundreds of fish and other creatures, circling and coalescing.

"Hello Prince Jayse, man of the north. I am Julta," the eel head said, nodding politely.

It wasn't the first time he'd heard a voice come from such a strange creature. The True Grannusians were notoriously shy, but on Nalanda Station, he'd had several chances to interact with them. That didn't make this any less special. "It's an honor," Jayse said.

"If you say so." Julta had a playful tone to his voice. "It's my understanding that there's been an incident here."

Jayse stared at the creature, thinking of everything the high chief had said. The man was close to declaring war on these people. If Jayse said too much, he could be named a traitor, a crime punishable by death, even for a prince. "My wife was kidnapped. We believe she was taken by Naiads."

The eel head tilted. "Really?"

Cathal lifted something that rested on the top of his bundle. He unwrapped a dark cloth to reveal a long knife with an elaborate handle. He showed it to Julta. "This was buried in a guard's chest near a Naiad's body. The Naiad was shot while trying to escape after the kidnapping. Do you recognize it?"

"How did you get that?" Jayse asked. He assumed that as it was evidence it would be locked up.

"Best not to ask," Cathal said with a wink.

Julta came forward, much of the eel's body rose out of the water. The school of fish below him lifted, twisting and turning together, taking on the vague shape of a torso. Some of the creatures weaved into an arm. His dark limb took the knife, examining it closer.

Each of the creatures in the lagoon, even those swimming at a distance, were connected to Julta. They were part of the True Grannusian. Like the cells in a human's body, they worked together to define a single being. When a True Grannusian came on dry land, they would wear an elaborate framework, a type of skeleton, outfitted with hydrating vessels, usually concealed under a robe.

Julta's voice was low and full of sorrow, looking at the knife. "I recognize the family markings. This belonged to a boy, a young man, I suppose, though he'd barely reached maturity. He was thought lost. His family has been desperate for weeks, trying to find him."

"Apparently, he became a kidnapper," Jayse snapped off.

"I seriously doubt it," Julta said.

Jayse wanted to answer back sharply, but he held his anger and asked, "What do you mean?"

Julta's dark eyes stared at Jayse. His gestures were too alien to interpret, but the prince got a sense of disapproval as he said, "You're judging them without ever meeting them. It would be best if you spoke to the Naiads directly. I think you will see all they want is to be left in peace."

Jayse pointed to the knife. "That was found in a guard's chest. That's not exactly peaceful."

Julta leaned his head forward and looked around at the towers of the palace. "And I'm sure in your surface world, things are always exactly how they seem." His dark eyes turned back to the prince. "If you wish to ask them about this, then I can arrange it."

"You would bring them here?" Jayse asked, noticing Cathal walking around the lagoon.

"Of course not. Your people are far too dangerous. As long as you promise you'll meet them without malice and keep your eyes open, I will bring you to a neutral spot, but I'll have nothing to do with it if you intend violence." The creatures that made up Julta's claw-like hand brought the knife back out, presenting it to Jayse. "In fact, you can return this to them. It will go a long way toward them trusting you."

He took the knife. "I just want my wife back." He tried to see what Cathal was doing. There was a set of controls by the gate. His friend was far enough away that Jayse would have to yell to be heard. He wanted to tell Cathal to stop, but he was already in motion, pulling a chain and lifting the portcullis manually.

The gate disappeared, climbing up into the wall. Then something passed through the opening. A soft glow below the water's surface lit the early morning, shining on the parts of Julta's body and lighting the rocks on the bottom of the lagoon. Cathal locked the chain off, leaving the gate open before coming back over.

"I've arranged transport for you," Julta said as a wide, shimmering creature approached. It broke the surface, looking like a large glowing soap bubble. Below it, tentacles dangled out, touching the sandy bottom.

Cathal came up to his friend. "It's not a short journey, but I packed us supplies," he said, indicating the bundle loaded with gear. He opened it, separating wetsuits, tanks, rebreathers, and fins. There was a small box with a battery pack and an air hose as well. He passed a dive mask to Jayse and nodded to the creature. "The cindaria can provide us with oxygen, but I thought you might prefer your own supply." He tapped the side of the machine.

"What?" Jayse asked. "We're going now? And that's our—"

"Our ride, yes. Look, you asked for my help." Cathal pointed into the lagoon. "This is it. I know you think I only came here because I had an agenda. But I am your friend, and I'm here for you. We're getting to the bottom of this, and we're getting your wife back."

Jayse took the mask. He looked at Julta, then at Cathal. Again, he debated over telling them what his father-in-law was planning, but he stayed quiet, going to the bundle and grabbing the wetsuit. "I appreciate the help..." His mouth stopped moving, though he had more to say. He wanted so badly to tell his friend they were on a clock. Instead, he asked, "How long will I be gone?"

"Two days out and two days back, if everything goes right," Cathal said.

Jayse's mouth fell open. "I can't be gone that long. What about Cormack? He's just lost one parent, and now, he's going to wake up and find the other one missing. I can't do that to him."

Cathal held up a tablet. "I understand, but things are moving quickly. Bad things. I think you know that."

Jayse stared at his friend with a question on his face, his eyebrow raised as he wondered what he knew. Cathal continued, "Tell the boy you've gone out to meet your father. Your people's ships are a day and a half out. Perhaps your absence will be enough to delay the high chief, to make him nervous." He handed the tablet to Jayse. "Remember, whatever you tell your son, the chief will hear as well."

Jayse chewed on his lip as he stared down at the device. His eyes went to the lagoon and the creature there. Its subtle glow would be noticed soon. Cathal wouldn't say it, but he knew as well that this little conspiracy could be discovered at any moment. Jayse nodded to himself and started recording.

"My little prince, don't be scared. I've decided to see your grandfather, my father. He's bringing his fleet here to Anchor Home. I promise I'll return to you, whatever it takes. I'll put our family back together. I love you, Cormack." He shut the device off before his emotions could overwhelm him, then he pulled on a wetsuit, with his face turned away from Cathal. When he was done, he wiped his tears, turned, and nodded to the creature in the lagoon, asking, "How exactly will that get us to... wherever we're going?"

"You'll see." Cathal smiled.

CHAPTER 9

There was a feeling of dread as the ocean pressed in on Jayse's wetsuit, and he stared out past the gate. Dawn wasn't far away. He wished he had time to go back and warn Cormack, to prepare his son for his absence. It broke his heart to think the boy would wake up without him, but this was the best chance to find his mother before things escalated. It had to be done in secret. If the high chief got word, Jayse couldn't guarantee the safety of the Naiads. The only person he risked this way was himself.

Cathal had brought three tanks for each of them. Three hours' worth of air under normal conditions but traveling in a cindaria was far from normal. They walked out into the lagoon as the creature moved into the deeper water near the gate. Cathal led the way, swimming down and bringing the tanks and gear up. Jayse watched from outside as his friend entered and left the glowing sphere. They both wore largynphone mics around their throats. The microphones detected vibrations in their vocal cords, allowing them to speak even with a mouthpiece in place. "Okay, come on in," Cathal said through comms.

With his dive mask on, and his rebreather in his mouth, Jayse dropped below the surface. He expected to come up into an open space inside the glowing creature, but it was a thicker medium, like jelly. "What is this?" he asked Cathal, looking at his friend who was blurry across the substance. Cathal wasn't on air. He pulled something like a vine, but less solid, down to his face.

"This is its insides. What did you expect? A luxury cabin?" Cathal asked, his voice sounding strange as the microphone built it from vibrations.

Jayse reached across, feeling the resistance. He touched the vine, noticing he could see through it. "And this, you're breathing through it?"

"Yeah, but I've something else for you," Cathal subvocalized, allowing the minimum amount of breath to pass over his vocal cords. He took the box with the air tube and powered it on. He attached it to Jayse's mask. The prince tried to ignore his friend tying the device into another vine. "It's a converter. You're still getting air from our friend here, but now, you can pretend you're not." He patted Jayse on the shoulder. "I know you can be a bit squeamish."

As the sun broke over the surface of the ocean, the cindaria passed through the gate. Below them, the sandy floor fell away. They stayed just above it, following the descent. Deeper and deeper they traveled into the dark, going far from the island of Anchor Home. A hundred meters down, the creature was like a single lantern floating in the vastness.

Outside its hazy walls, they saw Julta beside them as a school of fish, some large and some small. The variety of his parts made it hard to believe they were all fragments of the same species. When True Grannusians hatched from their eggs, in their larval state, they were all the same, but then, like organs in the body, they'd start to differentiate. Some stayed fish-like, while others grew claws and feet, developing strange crustacean attributes. Their size would vary too, with rumors of massive creatures that were still part of the Grannusian staying at a distance from the main hub.

Below them, the ocean floor hurried by as the cindaria's shape lengthened, pointing ahead. Its thicker tendrils were like jets, streaming water behind it. A day passed as they traveled above open fields of sand, then on the second day, plants of a thousand different varieties appeared. They grew in cracks and crevices, while strange fish swam by them in schools. Jayse had slept a good part of the journey, taking his mask off and loosening his wetsuit. The jelly inside the creature made him feel weightless. He never took his air pack off but never felt it as a burden either.

As he came alert, he wondered about the overwhelming drowsiness, if it was something in the jelly that made his eyes close, made the time pass, just as it was waking him now.

He thought to ask Cathal, but something caught his attention as he pulled his mask back down. He saw another source of light, glowing like a city in the distance. "What is that?" Jayse asked, pushing closer to the wall and trying to look out.

Cathal moved a little higher, looking over his friend's head. "That's Twilight, their capital."

Jayse never thought he'd see the main city of the Grannusians, but now that he was so close, the idea excited him. "Is that where we're meeting the Naiads?"

Cathal shook his head. "No, but we'll be close, just outside. . ."

Jayse couldn't be sure. It could've been the way the mic clicked off, leaving a delay, but there seemed to be something unsaid in the statement.

Below them was a seaweed grove with an open, sandy area in the center. The plants near the cleared spot glowed like landing lights. As the cindaria came down, its tentacles reached out, latching itself to stands of coral. They appeared random, but there were just enough to secure all its limbs. Julta moved something like a glowing root into the creature's interior. It was slow at first, but Jayse noticed the insides growing wider, pushing out like an expanding bubble.

The cindaria's jelly drained, forming a barrier below them, making a seal along the ocean floor. Jayse moved his hands more freely as his air bottle became heavy. He was still soaked in the jelly, but it dripped off him as the creature grew to a space eight meters around.

Cathal took the vine from his mouth and removed his dive mask. "You can come off air now," he said.

Jayse did as he was told, lifting his mask up, but leaving it on his head while the mouthpiece and regulator hung close by on his harness. He was tempted to take the bottle off, but he decided to leave it in place and to keep his flippers on his feet.

The walls of the cindaria were no longer hazy. They'd grown so thin that he wondered if they would continue to hold back the ocean. "This is incredible." He brought his hand up but hesitated to touch it. The world around him was a strange, alien landscape, a forest that swayed in the ocean currents, glowing with soft bioluminescence. It entranced him watching the stalks sway and the strange creatures come out. The fish and crabs, and animals with no human analogies were just as curious about him. There was too much life in too many forms to count. Then suddenly, anything that could swim darted away, back into the safety of the forest.

Something large shot by and drew his eyes up, moving like a high-speed train, both in speed and size. He caught only a glimpse, seeing a long, sinuous body, with shimmering scales of blue-green that nearly blended in with the water. A similar creature came from a different direction, barreling just as fast overhead. Then a third joined them. They twisted and danced across the ocean, soaring directly above Jayse. They moved the water and the walls of the cindaria, causing them to ripple as they cut through the ocean, leaving a rushing current in their wake.

Without being aware of it, Jayse stepped back. "Sea dragons!" he said, catching a glimpse of one of

their heads, seeing the long sharp teeth, the scales, and the pinpoint eyes that stared down at him with unnerving intelligence. At forty or fifty meters long, they made him feel incredibly small and fragile. They twisted and swam around each other, eventually slowing while circling the glowing sphere.

Dark forms dropped from their backs and swam down. The Naiads had arrived.

They moved through the water gracefully. Then, at the edge of the sphere, they dove low and pushed through the wall of jelly. They were on their feet in a single motion, moving their lithe bodies with ease.

The two men and one woman wore dark outfits, thinner than wetsuits, modestly covering them. Large openings on their backs revealed their grey skin and the gills that connected to their genetically engineered lungs. They wore harnesses on their hips and legs with small pouches and a long sheath for their knives.

Jayse noticed their dark eyes, too large for their faces, and sensed their wariness and distrust as they stood close to each other. He looked outside, seeing the dragons moving even slower. Their attention stayed on him and Cathal, ready to intervene for their masters.

The male Naiad in the front nodded to Cathal, who bowed in response, saying, "It's good to see you again, Nasir."

Nasir rubbed his chin and extended his hand. "I was surprised to hear from you so soon."

Cathal touched the back of his neck. "There have been some unfortunate developments. I'll tell you about it in a moment, but first, may I introduce you to my friend, Prince Jayse of the Tuisea clan, the people of the north, and husband to Dione of the Sidhe, the future high queen of the surface people."

Jayse raised an eyebrow and looked at his friend.
Cathal said bashfully, "Well, I want him to know
who he's talking to."

"So, this is the prince you told us about," Nasir
asked.

Cathal leaned toward Jayse, who stood with his
arms crossed. "I told them you were more reasonable
than most nobles. It was a compliment."

"Right." Jayse turned back to Nasir.

The Naiad's dark eyes stayed on the noble as he
said, "The Grannusians arranged a meeting with
Cathal, wanting to bridge the gap between our two
branches of humanity. We were wary but hopeful. Life
down here can be difficult, but we are happy with it.
Still, some, especially the young, wonder what it
would be like to know you, our cousins." Nasir
sounded only a little disapproving as he looked at the
female. Jayse noticed for the first time a family
resemblance between the two.

Nasir crossed his arms as well as he continued,
"Also, we hoped that someone like you, someone with
some level of power, could help protect my people.
There have been incidents. People who've gone
missing. We're left with terrible stories of what
happened to them."

Jayse sighed before saying, "That's actually why
I'm here." He kept his voice neutral. "We've had an
incident as well. My wife, the princess, has been
taken."

"I'm sorry to hear that." Nasir stared at him,
considering his expression. "You think we had
something to do with it? Why?"

Jayse nodded. "A Naiad was found in the palace.
It looked like he killed a guard before the guard
returned the favor."

The female Naiad stepped forward. "We would never! Only a fool would go anywhere near that island." She pointed her finger past him, toward Anchor Home. Jayse noticed behind her that one of the sea dragons had come closer. Its massive head was almost at the cindaria wall. Its mouth was closed, but Jayse could still see its teeth hanging over its bottom jaw. Bubbles came from its nose as its piercing eyes stared at him.

Nasir looked back, seeing the beast approach. He touched his daughter's shoulder. "Aysa, it's okay. We are here to talk. He's simply stating the facts. Not accusing us." His tone carried a hint of warning as he turned back to Jayse.

Cathal brought the knife out and offered it flat across his palms. "The guard had this buried in his chest."

Taking the blade, Nasir brought it close to his face, examining it. His expression went from curiosity to sadness, seeing the markings on the handle. He held it to the others in his group. The third member, the other male, brought his arms to his side, seeming to fold into himself at the sight. His hand went to his mouth.

Nasir watched his companion. He reached out and touched his arm, leaning in and whispering to him. The man's shoulders trembled. Nasir explained, his back turned to Jayse and Cathal, "This solves one mystery. But brings up so many other questions. The knife belonged to Talbert's son. His boy was curious, often going too close to your islands to get a peek at the surface world. He went missing a few weeks ago."

The man, Talbert, had a wet face as tears fell unheeded. He wiped them away and looked at his damp hand as if they were something strange. Taking a deep breath, he asked, "He was in the palace."

Cathal said, "Yes, his body was found down below in the sub-bays, the night the princess disappeared. The men who took her used a blow gun, like one of yours, to knock Jayse out."

"Could there be a rogue element amongst your people?" Jayse asked.

Nasir shook his head. "There are so few of us, and not many venture far from our colony. It's not safe, and it's a good distance from your city. Even getting here is a long journey. I can assure you; our numbers are accounted for. Talbert's son is the only one missing of late. His friends lost track of him near the mining equipment in the western sea."

Jayse turned to Cathal and asked, "What mining equipment?"

Cathal raised an eyebrow, surprised that Jayse didn't know. "They're going ahead with the volcanism project. Has no one told you? The high chief started digging using your people's technology. It's been going on for months. Your tribe is helping him."

Jayse's face turned red with embarrassment. He took a small step back, shaking his head. "What? I mean, I knew they were talking about it, but I had no idea they'd gone ahead."

Cathal pointed out to the ocean where Julta's school was slowly circling. "That's why the True Grannusians have been so scarce at the capital. Much of the ambassadorial staff left in protest."

Jayse wondered if his wife knew. 'Of course she did,' he thought, answering his own question, while his eyes followed Cathal's hand, gesturing out into the dark water. He shook his head and smiled painfully as he looked past Julta and the sea dragons, feeling like a fool. Something caught his attention. Above them was a shadow in the distance, a black spot against the nearly unperceivable sunlight.

He squinted and asked, "What is that?" as he noticed how agitated Julta had become. The Grannusian crashed a number of his components into the sphere's wall, trying to warn them about the dark thing that loomed above them.

"It's an attack sub!" Nasir turned sharply toward the two surface dwellers. "You've betrayed us!?"

"No, never," Cathal said.

Grabbing his mask and pulling it back over his face, Jayse yelled, "Get down!" He saw two lines of bubbles streaking through the water, following torpedoes aimed at them.

The sea dragon scattered before the weapons as they came rocketing into the grove. They exploded just outside the cindaria, breaching its thin walls. They dissolved in the blast, letting the sea flood in. The nearby coral blew apart, sending shrapnel along with a cloud of sand into the water. It cut Jayse's flesh, blowing him back.

The ocean slammed down on him, smashing him to the ground as the pressure wave pummeled his whole body. Only the earpieces for the comms saved his eardrums from destruction.

"Jayse!" Cathal's broken voice called over comms. His friend was swimming down, back toward their gear that was spread across the bottom. The prince had no idea how he'd ended up so far above, but he realized that Cathal hadn't been as quick getting his breathing apparatus to his face. He shook his head, trying to clear it as he swam down.

'Where are the others,' he wondered as debris floated around him. He grabbed Cathal's leg, saying,

"I'm here," while dragging him back. Tugging at his arm and shoulder, he turned Cathal until he could touch his naked face, then he took his own mouthpiece and shoved it past his friend's lips.

Cathal still wore a tank on his back, but the regulator was damaged, and his mask was nowhere to be found. There was little chance he saw anything other than a cloudy figure. As he filled his lungs, Jayse searched the bottom. Their gear was scattered across the ocean floor while chunks of the cindaria floated by. He was tempted to go hunting for equipment, but he knew they were only targets while they were out here, so he swam toward the wall of plants.

He hadn't seen the Naiads do the same. The three ducked into the forest, using the cover to get closer to the sub. When they were directly below it, they emerged, swimming up faster than a surface person ever could. The three sea dragons had gone far in opposite directions to avoid the torpedoes, but like a pack of wolves, they never let their prey out of their sight. With long, sinuous twists of their bodies, one after the other, they turned in and blazed a path through the water, diving below their masters. The Naiads grabbed hold of their backs, gripping tight to thin harnesses as the beasts climbed, charging the sub.

The mid-class vessel, thirty meters long, had a crew of twelve men. It had no windows or lights. It saw through a sensor package that detected heat, sound, and movement of the water. More bubble trails came from it as it fired again, sending torpedoes targeted at the dragons.

The creatures broke away again in different directions. They avoided the weapons with ease before turning back, closing in even faster this time. With their thick skulls and muscular bodies, one, then another, and another smashed into the sub, tossing the dark thing out of position. They turned again for another attack run.

Below, Jayse and Cathal were busy scurrying along the edge of the clearing. Staying inside the forest of plants, Jayse searched for the gear bag of spare equipment. He couldn't get far from Cathal as they were still sharing air, handing the mouthpiece back and forth. He found the bag half-buried beneath the settling sand.

Tugging it back to them, he searched inside. He found a mask and passed it to Cathal. His original was unlikely to be recovered. As Cathal pulled it over his face, along with a new regulator, he turned and looked at the prince. His eyes went wide seeing Jayse. The prince glanced down and realized why. Blood was seeping from his body, clouding the water. He'd felt the sting of cuts from the blown-apart coral, but with adrenaline coursing through him, he didn't realize how bad the bleeding was.

"We've got to do something about that," Cathal said.

"You're hurt too," Jayse pointed out, seeing the way Cathal was holding his arm.

They both looked in the direction of the Grannusian city glowing in the distance. "That's a long way to go with you leaving a trail." Cathal studied their surroundings warily. The risk of bleeding out was one thing, but the chance of attracting a predator was far more concerning. Already, several fish were circling his torso. When he felt one touch him, he pushed it away.

"Don't." Cathal grabbed his arm. "It's Julta." He pointed to the large eel, emerging from a nearby stand of kelp. Jayse held his hands in the air and let them gather closer, squeezing over his wounds and trying to staunch the flow of blood.

They both looked up, hearing the sound of explosions and feeling the pressure waves. Blooms of vaporized water formed like deadly clouds around the sub. The torpedoes were set for close detonation, trying to hit the dragons as they repeatedly swept in, smashing into its side.

Blood wept from one of the dragons, the result of rapidly firing flechettes, shot from turrets on the sub's hull. The weapons tracked the creatures, trying to keep them back, but the speed of the beasts and the way they twisted and turned was nearly impossible to track.

Another torpedo launched, but just as it cleared the tube, the dragon ridden by the female Naiad, Aysa, weaved in, passing dangerously close to the weapon. Its tail slapped the torpedo, sending it back. It exploded a short distance from the vessel, blowing the housing off the sub's propellers. There was the sound of shearing metal as the blades ripped apart, sending deadly shrapnel through the water.

The sub started to fall at a strange angle. It rolled starboard while bubbles appeared above it. The hull was cracked, and the precious air was escaping.

The dragons didn't give up their assault. They came back for the kill, relentlessly ramming into the vessel, sending it faster toward the bottom. The dark thing crashed into the glowing forest, uprooting the vegetation in a long swath.

The dragons moved in slowly now. Their long bodies touched the bottom as they used their massive teeth to tear at the metal and widen the opening in its side. The sub's occupants wore pressure suits and helmets in preparation for a breach, but that did little to protect them from outraged sea monsters.

When the crack was wide enough, the dragons took turns jamming their heads in the broken side. Their muzzles were long, searching past the shell, looking for flesh. They pulled the men from the sub, rending limbs and grinding bodies in half.

Jayse watched in horror, too distracted to notice a subtle pull at his waist. Julta was moving him, gently swimming him up and away from the scene of destruction, heading toward the lights in the distance. More dark spots were closing in. They were large creatures, a little like oversized shrimp with a Grannusian swarm around each of them. More cindaria came as well, glowing like a string of lanterns. It was a rescue team from the city of Twilight. They closed in, some going to Jayse and Cathal and others going to the sub.

The dragons pushed back against the approaching Grannusians, allowing the schools to surround them and tend to their wounds in the same way they had tended to Jayse's. Gently, Julta brought him into a cindaria with Cathal close behind him. The jelly-like insides no longer felt strange but were soothing against his wounds. As Julta continued to treat him, the creature started on its way back to Twilight, the city of the Grannusians.

CHAPTER 10

"Open your eyes. You're about to see something special," Cathal said through the mic. Jayse didn't realize his eyes had closed, and that exhaustion had momentarily overtaken him. The blood loss was stopped with Julta closing up the cuts in his flank. He touched the wounds and felt a waxy firmness where coral had sliced him. The upper half of his wetsuit was in tatters, but he left it on anyway, knowing how cold the ocean could be at this depth.

He felt his friend's touch as he pushed him through the gel, closer to the wall of the cindaria to see. The city of Twilight was laid out in natural crevices and valleys along the ocean's bottom. Nothing like a human city, it was built of transparent columns that turned and twisted, reflecting the cindaria glow in strange hues as they followed the sea bed, rising and diving. Some glass-like structures climbed high, pointing to the surface, while others dove down and disappeared into the rocks.

Alive with activity, the city had thousands of Grannusians swimming about in their schools, both large and small, above a central valley, like a bowl of rock candy. At every turn, there were more plants and animals attached to the transparent walls. It was impossible to tell that their growth was purposeful, with each living thing fulfilling a function.

Jayse wondered if any were weapons. Over the centuries, more than one uninvited guest from the surface had been turned away from Twilight. They were sent back above with no memory of how they lost their vessels.

Jayse thought of his father-in-law and wondered if that would be his fate as well. Would he be gently returned to his palace with no knowledge of his foolishness?

The cindaria came down to a large crystal chamber. It passed through a barrier that at first seemed solid but turned permeable as they approached. Several of the creatures followed Jayse and Cathal, carrying the surviving crew of the sub. Cathal told Jayse over the Mic. "We've got to swim up. There's air in the chamber above."

"How do you know that?"

"Because I've been here before. Come on," he said, diving down, passing through the cindaria's bottom half. Its tentacles spread apart, latching to the wall. Jayse exited and found a platform just above the water's edge. Cathal helped him climb out with his heavy scuba gear. As he did, the gel from the cindaria dripped away, dissolving in the water. The platform was twenty meters squared and barren, with a few blocks carved from a glass-like material, near the wall. Jayse looked back out through the reddish tint of the walls and ceiling at the city. Coming from above, the sea dragons dove down, entering the chamber.

The sound of people surfacing in the pool drew Jayse's attention. Three men climbed out, aided by the cindaria and by several schools of Grannusians, one of which was Julta.

Cathal didn't approach the sailors, and he indicated by holding up his hand that Jayse should stay back as well. He said to his friend, "Go ahead and strip your gear." Both men watched the survivors.

The sailors wore dark, unmarked clothing with harnesses and small air tanks on their chests. Their faces were hidden behind reflective faceplates. They were still slick from the cindaria. Before they could do anything aggressive, their uniforms melted away.

Judging by their response, it was unexpected. Their belts fell to the ground and their pressure suits as well. Even their helmets dissolved, cracking and falling, revealing three confused men, left uncomfortably naked.

Jayse immediately dropped his scuba tank. "That's not about to happen to us, is it?"

Cathal shook his head. "No." He looked back at Jayse. "I mean, I don't think so."

"It won't," Julta said from the water. "But I'd still suggest avoiding aggressive behavior."

Cathal opened his mouth to speak, but before he got a word out, a large head covered in glistening scales, nearly twice the height of a man, emerged from the water. Two more followed. The sea dragons soaked the platform, splashing as they emerged and cleared their airways. They sprayed water everywhere as their eyes glinted, looking over the men.

There was nowhere to run if the creatures decided to attack. The men from the sub backed away, going to the far wall. Jayse moved as well, staring at the long teeth and the nearest creature's partially open mouth. He wondered if the chunks of the men it'd pulled from the sub were still there, jammed against its gums.

He felt Cathal reach out to him, shaking him from his fearful trance. "It's fine," he said.

"Is it?" someone called. The first dragon turned, revealing the female Naiad, Aysa. She was half in the water, holding a leather harness. "Because I'm not sure this wasn't a trap. That you two didn't plan the whole thing."

Jayse motioned to his wounds. "Yes, I planned to be blown halfway across the ocean. That was the point of this whole thing. Boy, did I get you."

"You're far from your kingdom, Prince," the girl threatened as the dragon's head came closer.

"Aysa, calm yourself," her father said from the back of his own beast. He brought it close to the platform and stepped off. As he looked at the naked men, he unsheathed his knife. "These are the ones we need to press. They know what happened to Talbert's son." The third dragon, the one carrying Talbert, came over. He stepped next to Nasir and pulled his knife as well; his face was locked with rage as he closed in.

The survivors stood against the wall, and despite what happened to their companions, they didn't cower. They stayed alert, never taking their eyes from the dragons or their riders. They each prepared to fight with their hands up and their shoulders squared to their attackers. They weren't just soldiers, Jayse realized, but men like Cathal, who'd been in bad situations before. He didn't envy the position they were in, but he respected their sureness.

With the sound of splashing, Julta forced his eel head nearly out of the water. "Nasir, our directive against violence doesn't only apply to surface people. You know this."

Nasir held paused like a tiger ready to pounce, eyeing the three men, while Talbert continued forward. Julta asked, "Are you going to force a response?"

Nasir reached out and grabbed the other Naiad, stopping him. Talbert grunted and pushed his knife back in its sheath as his daughter called, "But they tried to kill us."

"I know, Aysa; I was there, but here in Twilight, you're safe." Julta looked at the survivors. "And you are safe as well. For now."

"But who are they?" Cathal asked, taking a few steps toward the men. His posture wasn't aggressive, just curious.

Julta pointed out, "That is the most important question, isn't it?"

"And how did they follow us here?" Jayse asked. "We need to know that as well."

"That is more obvious," Julta said. "It was you."

"I knew it," Aysa snapped. Her dragon responded to her anger, sweeping in close to the platform. Jayse jumped back, going close to the naked soldiers.

"Hold girl!" Nasir called to his daughter.

Julta explained, "It wasn't on purpose. The prince isn't aware he has a tracker inside him, that he is being monitored. I would say it was placed while you were unconscious after the dart, though it could've been inside you much longer."

"How do you know that?" Jayse asked.

Julta nodded to Jayse's wounds, then to the cindaria. "When we heal or when you travel that way, you are part of something larger. We can see all of you."

"Did you know before the meeting?" Cathal asked.

It was the first time Julta looked surprised. "Yes." He nodded.

"And you didn't tell us," Aysa asked.

Julta didn't seem to want to answer at first, but then he said, "I'm sorry. I wasn't expecting them to attack you. We thought they were spying, not that they'd attempt to assassinate their own." He nodded to Jayse.

"Wait, they're own, what do you mean?" Cathal took a step away from the wall, glancing back at the men.

"I think someone wants to keep you from investigating your wife's disappearance."

"Why?" Jayse demanded, though he immediately thought of his father-in-law, of his plans, and all the royals he gathered to his cause.

"Let's find out," Julta said, turning to the soldiers. "Who are you people? What master do you serve?"

The three men looked at each other briefly. One stepped forward and said, "We've nothing to tell you."

"I doubt that," Aysa said, closing in with her dragon again. Its head came down on the platform, meters from the front man. "I'll get them to talk," she promised.

"That won't be necessary," Julta assured her, looking down into the pool. His school of fish brought something to the surface. They pushed a frame over the wall's edge, then followed it, wrapping around the device that was vaguely in the shape of a man. The different pieces squirmed and tightened around the structure, and the eel's head wiggled to the top.

This was the Grannusian form Jayse was most familiar with, what the steward and professors on Nalanda looked like, though they usually wore a robe over their strange bodies, out of a sense of decorum for the students. The framework and the body of the creature working without cover was an odd sight. Julta walked toward the men, pushing the dragon back with a single, gentle gesture. Aysa looked surprised at how the creature responded as she rode it back into the pool. Its head went under, and she swam back up, going to join the other Naiads, leaning in a whispering to them.

All eyes were on Julta as, with a squishing, slippery sound, he closed in on the survivors. His gate was lurching as he struggled to control all the little bodies that made him up. He reached out to the first man, who tried to push the strange arm away and pull back, avoiding the Grannusian's reach.

There was nowhere to go, with his companions already backed up to the wall. The man tried ducking below Julta, but the Grannusian grabbed his shoulder and pulled him to his feet. It was impossible to see the tiny needles that appeared from Julta's claw-like hand, but as he wrapped it around the man's other arm and closed tightly, they pierced his flesh.

The man let loose an utterance of pain. He tried to control it, not let his enemies know just how much the needles hurt. He gritted his teeth, then his face relaxed, and his eyes rolled back in his head. Julta watched and asked, "You will answer my question, won't you?"

The man resisted a second more, shaking his head. His body nearly collapsed, but Julta held him up. Finally, he stuttered out the words, "We are in the service... the service of the Duke Takia of the Tuisea clan, second to Chief Balif of the north."

Jayse felt his spine turn to ice as he heard his father's name. He took a step forward as Cathal's hand fell on his shoulder. "You serve my father?" Jayse asked.

The man's eyes stayed down, focusing on nothing. "We serve the first duke. Your father's cousin."

Jayse heard the Naiads whispering to each other. Aysa was accusing them again, but he ignored her. He swallowed hard, afraid to ask a question, but he had to have the answer, knowing it could change his entire life. Julta glanced back and waved him forward. He knew what Jayse was thinking. Jayse shook off Cathal's hand and stepped next to the Grannusian. He ignored the squishing sounds of the creature's body and asked the survivor, "Does my father know what you were up to? What your duke is doing?"

The two other survivors tried to stop him from giving away more information. They pushed forward, but a low roar from the nearest dragon kept them at bay.

Jayse stared at the man, whose head was still cast down while his eyes remained unfocused, rolling about in his head. He said in a low voice, like a rumbling exhale, "There are others... but Chief Balif isn't one." Jayse sighed, feeling relief, but then the man added, "If he gets in the way, he will be gone. He won't leave Anchor Home."

That cold feeling in Jayse's spine melted, turning hot as he thought of his father, a man who he knew to be honorable. He was angry that his time in the capital, around men whose morality was for sale, had ever led him to question his father. He was nearly certain of the answer but asked one more question anyway, "The high chief knows, doesn't he?"

"Yes," the survivor said. "But he's not the one who sent us. We came from Deep's Blade, from the duke."

Jayse's father-in-law was bringing together an armada, preparing for war. He must've sent word to the duke. Glancing at Cathal, he realized that the moment he left Anchor Home, with the tracker inside him, the high chief decided he was a traitor. That attack sub was there for him. If he went home, his fate would be grim. There would be no trial. He'd be shuffled off, placed in some dark place while the war began. The high chief would probably even find some way to blame his wife's kidnapping on him, say that he was in collusion with the Naiads. He looked at Cathal, and for a moment, he was tempted to blame him, but he shook his head, knowing that wasn't fair. This began with his wife's kidnapping, and his mission was still the same. Find her, and then he could worry about finding a way home. He looked at the man, knowing there was one more question to ask. "Where is my wife?"

The man tried to resist again. He shook his head, but Julta squeezed, putting more chemicals into his system. "She's with the duke. He took her."

CHAPTER 11

'What now?' was the question on everyone's lips, though the answer was obvious to Jayse; the 'how' concerned him. Duke Takia was the warden of the northern tribes, a posting made for violent times when tribes fought over resources and honor. He controlled a string of fortifications at the very edge of the northern territory, including a stronghold on a true island.

Unlike Anchor Home, the castle, Deep's Blade, was on a tiny piece of land, the tallest point of an underwater mountain range. It was the southernmost point of the Northern territory where icebergs touched warm currents, melted, and died. Unfortunately, it was almost five thousand kilometers away. Even for the swift cindaria, it would take days to get there, and for the sea dragons, it would be even longer. Jayse couldn't be sure what the Naiads intended. They knew now who was responsible for the death of Talbert's son, a noble who they'd never heard of and the high chief of the surface world. Aysa wanted revenge, but the other two, the elders, said little about what they intended.

Julta didn't seem bothered by the distance. While Nasir pleaded for patience with his daughter, who wanted to leave right away, find the two leaders and take blood for blood, Julta promised a solution.

He excused himself as other Grannusians joined him on the platform. They reached out to the survivors from the sub. Quelling their resistance, they injected them like the first one. The men became willing thralls, and the Grannusians guided them into the pool where a cindaria waited.

As Jayse watched the soldiers following like children, he asked, "What do you plan to do with them?"

Julta explained, "We recovered a life raft from the sub. It will be brought to the surface along with these men. They will be placed in it with no memory of these events."

The Grannusians left while Jayse and Cathal stayed behind with the Naiads. Strange creatures that emerged from the pool and wiggled across the floor brought them food and fresh water contained in gourds. They looked like tongues broken free from a giant's mouth.

Cathal and two older Naiads took advantage of the refreshments while Jayse looked on. It wasn't until Cathal warned him that, "You'll need your strength for what comes next," that he finally ate some of the oysters and drank the water. He didn't realize until then how famished he was.

Everyone but Aysa sat on the glass blocks, gathering around like they were at a picnic. She stayed by her dragon, petting its side, ignoring the humans and the two older men from her species.

"Those soldiers, that sub was here to kill me," Jayse said to his friend, "I can't go back to Anchor Home."

"I know," Cathal said.

Jayse's voice was shaking, "How will I see my son again?"

Cathal reached over and touched his friend's arm. "By bringing your wife back. By exposing this whole conspiracy. The high chief is playing a dangerous game. He needs to be stopped."

"You honestly think my wife will help bring down her father?" Jayse asked. "How would that even work?"

Cathal assured him, "She'll do it. Your wife is stronger than you think."

Jayse shook his head. "I still don't understand. Why did he need all this to start a war?"

Cathal looked at him, his eyes going wide. Jayse added, "Yes, he all but told me that's what he's intending." He motioned toward Twilight. "I think he's planning on attacking the True Grannusians."

Nasir and Talbert were staring at them, shocked by what they heard.

"Well, that's just stupid." Cathal shrugged and laughed a little. He leaned closer and said, "Look, there's always rumblings among the other chiefs. His alliances aren't as strong as they seem, not for what he wants." He pointed to the Naiads, then rolled his eyes back to the city. "But we both know that there's more at stake than just the people we share this planet with. Think back to who else was in that room."

Jayse stared at his friend, wondering again how much he knew. He was about to ask him about Tamerlane's fleet when Cathal added, "We have to expose this little game. It's the only way to keep everyone safe. It's the only way you get back to Cormack."

Nasir called, "Even if you bring this Chief down, it'll still go on for us. Humans have never needed an excuse to destroy what is different from them. It is a flaw in our DNA."

Jayse looked at his strange, grey skin and large, black eyes. Despite their differences, the Naiads still considered themselves human. They hadn't traveled that far from their origin.

Talbert's head was down. He was looking at his son's knife. "If there is a way, I will help you see your son again," he promised, bringing his dark eyes up to stare at Jayse. "I may've lost mine, but I promise I will help you see yours again."

Jayse tried to think of all the reasons this stranger would be willing to help him. There was logic in it, of course, but somehow, Jayse knew that wasn't the reason Talbert offered his assistance. "Thank you," he said. "And I promise, I will do all I can to make these people pay."

A little distance off, Aysa laughed. "There is only one way that happens. Are you willing to do it?" She called.

Nasir said to her, "We're not looking for more blood."

Aysa laughed again, bitterly shaking her head. "Maybe you're not."

Nasir touched Talbert's shoulder and explained to Cathal and Jayse, "She and Talbert's son were in love, young love, the most fiery kind." He leaned in and whispered, "As a father, I'm worried about her. I know she won't be stopped."

As Aysa continued to pet her dragon with her back to the men, Cathal said, "I almost feel bad for them." The four men said little else, but they all seemed to understand that they were in this together. Then, a massive, dark thing came overhead.

The top of the chamber was transparent, as were all the walls, with only a slightly reddish tint, but now, the surface had gone dark as a shadow came over, covering a quarter of the city. "What is that?" Jayse asked, his head leaning far back.

"I don't know," Cathal said.

"It's Julta's solution." Talbert shook his head, a smile breaking across his face.

Nasir turned to his friend. "He called one from the depths?"

"Called what from the depths?" Jayse asked.

Nasir's voice was amused. "You should know. Your people build farms and colonies on their corpses. It's the leviathan."

Jayse saw it now, the edges of a shell, not so different from a turtle's, only so much larger. The creature was a kilometer wide, with dozens of fins, the size of spaceships, moving like cilia along its side. The shape of its head was like the peak of a mountain with long lines of baleen, massive filters, standing as tall as buildings in its three mouths. It had no eyes, but long stalks of sensors, glowing like streetlamps, dangling from its head, there to detect cliff walls down in the ocean's depths.

No one noticed Julta returning, not until a particularly large cindaria surfaced in the pool. "Your ride awaits," Julta said, swimming next to it. "The cindaria will attach to the leviathan, and you'll travel on its belly to the northern territory."

Aysa stood by her dragon. The three creatures stared up at the leviathan as well as she asked, "What about our dragons?"

Julta considered the creatures who weren't far from him in the pool. Their heads alone were so much larger than him. "It'd be better if they stayed here. But I suppose they could try to ride above, on its shell. I worry that if they fall off, they won't be able to keep up, and if they get caught in its wash, it could be a rough turn."

Nasir shook his head. "If there's another fight, I'd rather have them with me. I will take them, but I'll guide them alone. The others should ride in the cindaria."

Aysa began to protest, but her father silenced her.

Cathal pointed at the leviathan. "This is great, and I really appreciate it, but where we're going isn't the most welcoming place. It's a well-outfitted military installation, and this isn't exactly stealthy. Five people, a couple of dragons, and even a leviathan can't fight the army they've got there. We'll need to get inside without a lot of fuss."

Talbert asked Jayse, "Hasn't this man sworn fealty to your father? Shouldn't he welcome you?"

"The man who probably kidnapped my wife? I doubt it," Jayse said.

"True." Talbert nodded.

Cathal looked at the spot where the survivors from the sub had their uniforms melt away. "Is there any more gear on the sub? Or was everything destroyed?"

Julta nodded. "I'll see." Then he swam off.

CHAPTER 12

A short time later, Talbert, Aysa, Jayse, and Cathal swam into the cindaria. Between the distance and the condenser not surviving the attack, Jayse had no choice but to use the creature's air. Through his dive mask, he watched Cathal settle one of the vines into his mouth, then followed his example. It slipped past his soft palate, settling uncomfortably just behind his tongue.

Using the creature's air supply came with other benefits. The cindaria could regulate the release of nitrogen in their tissue, aiding in decompression as they ascended to reach the fortress. Julta, with the aid of the Naiads, recovered a few air bottles and three uniforms from the sub, all fitted for males, which didn't make Aysa happy. Only Talbert, Cathal, and Jayse would be making entry.

Julta also found flechette pistols. The Grannusian had pushed the armored boxes toward them with obvious disgust. Their species didn't claim to be pacifist. Certainly, they'd defend themselves if they were attacked, but weapons were strictly forbidden in Twilight.

They took the pistols but knowing the place, Cathal warned against itching for a fight. "It'd be better if we could get in and out without making any trouble."

Nasir and Talbert agreed, but Aysa didn't seem the type to listen. Cathal's special forces team had been deployed from the fortress in the past, and he'd taken the time while there to gauge its weaknesses. He knew of a moon pool in its lower level, large enough for several subs to surface, but there were other passages, natural caverns left over from volcanic activity. Most had been blocked off, but he thought he could find a frail point, hoping one of the openings' mortar had become weakened by the ocean water. Hearing his plan, Julta promised the cement wouldn't be a problem. He gave Cathal several organic sacks full of chemicals that he said would help.

The cindaria swam up to the leviathan. It turned slowly so that its tentacles and the opening at its bottom could attach to the larger creature's belly. The top of the leviathan, the main part of the shell, had a sail and smaller fixed fins that Nasir thought the dragons could use to hold on to. He waved goodbye to his daughter and guided the beasts above as the leviathan slowly began its journey. As it left the lights of Twilight behind, it sped up. Hundreds of fins like the oars on an ancient warship stroked the water, cutting through it. Below, the cindaria warped, compressing the passengers' space as the four laid themselves flat.

Jayse and Cathal still had their mics around their throats. Though it felt rude, it afforded them their first chance to speak in private. "Are you okay?" Cathal asked his friend.

Jayse found speaking with the vine in his mouth nearly impossible. He started and stopped several times before he managed to get out a garbled message, "How, how is this going to go? Takia controls a legion. What chance do we have?" He swallowed, hating the feel of the thing in his mouth. "And if we're successful, what happens next? What will my wife actually do about her father and his plans?"

"Let's worry about the first part first, yes? And you've got me for that. You're already off to a good start." The microphones didn't pick up Cathal's tone, and he couldn't smile with the vine in his mouth, but he patted Jayse on the shoulder. Then his eyes went to

Aysa, who was next to him, as he added, "I'm worried too but just follow my lead, and we'll be fine."

Jayse noticed Talbert and Aysa's hands moving. They tried not to make it obvious, but they were communicating as well. Living underwater, their people had an entire language in gestures. He thought of how they'd entered the chamber in Twilight and stood in the air, and how they'd spoken common. Yes, they could breathe water, but they weren't dependent on it.

He shouldn't be surprised. This form of humanity wasn't a natural development, but something engineered by the True Grannusians, a gift to humanity, one rejected by those clinging to the surface.

Jayse thought of the old stories, of the time when people first made their home on this world. They said they came from Tairnish, an inhospitable, barren moon where man was barely able to survive. The Grannusians had helped there as well, engineering people who could live in that terrible place. Today, the Tairnish took pride in their strength and even in the strange pigment on their skin that helped block radiation.

They had little choice. But here, humanity managed to cling to the few rocks sticking above the waves and to the hollowed-out shells of these massive creatures. The human population had grown enough on the surface that they could turn their noses up at those who chose to adapt. Their bloodlines separated, but the surface dwellers and Naiads were still the same species, one above and one below.

Occasionally, he'd heard stories of surface women giving birth to Naiad children. A genetic remnant from when the two branches weren't so far apart.

Traditionally, those children were returned to the sea, cast into the waves as babies, pariahs who barely knew life. He looked at Aysa, knowing her father was above. Thinking of his own son, Jayse wondered at the cruelty of such a taboo.

Hours passed, but they were still a good distance from the fortress when underwater mountain ranges appeared. Rocky outcroppings rose from the deep and nearly touched the surface, forcing the leviathan to slow its headlong rush.

Cathal's dive mask stayed locked on the cindaria's thin wall, trying to understand where they were. After a long while, he said, "We're close," noticing landmarks that meant nothing to the others.

He touched Talbert's arm and pointed to the bottom of the leviathan, where the cindaria clung, indicating it was time to break free. Talbert wore a fleshy polyp over one of his arms with smaller tentacles climbing toward his neck. He reached out, pushing the covered arm along the seal. The touch appeared gentle, but it was enough to tell the creature to release.

The cindaria dropped suddenly away, falling from the leviathan, spinning in the creature's wash. As it rolled again and again, the passengers felt its body contracting, pulling water into transparent organs and jetting it out again, trying to stabilize itself. Jayse gripped his vine to keep from being thrown around in the jelly. He smacked against Cathal, then Talbert, and Aysa. When the cindaria finally settled again with its tentacles pointed down, its body returned to a round form, giving the passengers a bit more space.

Cathal had caught the air tanks in the chaos, hugging them to himself. He was bringing the gear back together as the cindaria leveled off. It rose above the leviathan's back so they could look down on the city-sized creature.

With the speed of a hurtling train, the massive creature never stopped moving, barreling into the dark ocean, an island disappearing in the distance. The sail on its back sliced through the water as everyone's eyes searched the shell. There was no sign of the sea dragons or Nasir.

A flurry of hand gestures passed between Talbert and Aysa while her face twisted with concern. She slapped his shoulder and pointed back where they'd come from. Talbert shook his head, making it clear that they didn't have time to go back.

Not wanting to interrupt, Cathal inched slowly forward through the jelly. He touched Talbert on the arm to get his attention. Aysa whipped her head around. Her dark eyes and face twisted in anger as Talbert nodded to Cathal, who pointed into the depths.

A narrow canyon ran between the mountains, a black place like a crooked pencil line. Cathal motioned for them to dive. Then he gestured ahead at a peak that climbed above the other mountains. It was a wall of rock, the true island with a fortress on it.

Talbert nodded. He went past Aysa, taking his covered hand and moving it down along the cindaria's outer wall. The creature started to descend toward the pass. Before long, in the glow from the cindaria, claustrophobic walls closed in around them.

Everywhere they looked, jagged stone edges reached out like the dark fingers of giants. Closer though, there was life, anemones and worms searching with colorful appendages that danced in the wake of their passage, waiting for their next meal to come too close. Just above the floor, the cindaria twisted and pulled its body in, trying to avoid being ripped by the ledges. Jayse was left to wonder, not for the first time, about the creature's intelligence.

While everyone else minded the walls, Aysa's attention stayed above. Looking back, she kept watch for her father and the Dragons. Jayse glanced back when he felt Cathal touch his shoulder. He pointed at shadows high above. "Those are mines. That's why we're going this way."

"I suppose it's safer down here?" Jayse asked.

"I hope so." Cathal shrugged.

CHAPTER 13

The walls moved away as they reached the far end of the passage. They began to rise, and Cathal stayed by the cindaria's outer barrier, searching the dark, cinder walls formed a thousand years before by this world's boiling heart. The volcanic rock was pockmarked with shallow openings and some that were deeper.

Above them, they saw the shadow of structures where the fortress hung out over the ocean, past the island's edge. Navigation lights showed the way for submarines, leading them to the docks in the large moon pool. Only a single silhouette was there now, one small sub tied up in a space large enough for a hundred-meter-long attack vessels. Technicians and soldiers moved like ants in the bright lights. Jayse worried they'd see the cindaria's glow, but the creature had dampened, only shining softly.

"There," Cathal said, pointing at a deep cavity in the wall above them. Jayse could see a lighter material inside it. The smooth surface of the man-made plug was made from a type of concrete.

Cathal motioned with his hand for Talbert to stop the cindaria's ascent. He swam down in the gel and opened the weapon's box. Four pistols were packed neatly together with the flechettes cartridges stored next to them. Cathal loaded them and passed out three to the men going inside. Before he could close the box again, Aysa took out the last. Cathal stared at her, but as they couldn't speak with each other, it was impossible to argue. She motioned with her hand, waving for the ammo. Reluctantly, Cathal passed it up. He shook his head, watching her load it as he had.

Next, he tied an air bottle into a pack and pulled it on. The men on the sub had worn full helmets with heads-up displays inside. He pulled one of these on as well and attached the regulator.

Jayse helped Talbert with his gear. He was already in a wetsuit, but he'd left it unzipped and half pulled down so as not to cover his gills. The gear was strange to the Naiad, having never depended on anything to breathe underwater. Jayse watched him pull the helmet on. It hid his eyes behind a flat visor with small sensor holes and his face with a breathing apparatus.

While it was all practical, the mask served a second purpose. The man inside was no longer an individual. He was a soldier, like the man next to him, no longer responsible for the orders he followed.

They became men who would break into a home and steal a mother, men who would wipe out a species of humans for being different, not villains, though; those were men like his father-in-law. As he got his gear on, he thought of Tamerlane's fleet cruising from Uppsala to the colonies in the ring. The people there were as different from regular humans as these Naiads. They'd been warped by generations living in low gravity, in the only homes open to them. If they went anywhere else, the gravity would crush them.

Tamerlane called them squatters and criminals. Jayse had never seen an Uppsalan soldier in person, but he'd studied images in his military training. He knew their helmets were mirror-like face shields with no eyes. The only thing their victims would see was their own reflection looking back at them.

Jayse pulled his helmet on and attached the air pack to the regulator, then he followed Cathal and Talbert out of the cindaria. Though Aysa wasn't going in, she came out into the water and stayed back, watching them.

Cathal led the way, moving easily in the gear. He climbed the wall with his feet dangling out behind him until the light of his helmet found the opening and the plug. Working quickly, he placed one of the chemical-filled bulbs on the surface and pierced it with his knife. A viscous material seeped free, drifting a little in the water. Using the blade, he spread it out.

Bubbles rose from the surface, then Cathal used the blade again. He pushed it into the concrete mortar, jamming through the softening material. In moments, he pulled away large chunks of stone, clearing the small volcanic tunnel. He looked at his knife, making sure it was still sharp. Whatever the chemical was, it seemed to only affect the mortar. He looked back once at the others, then disappeared inside. Talbert went next, then Jayse. The prince glanced at Aysa, who floated beside the cindaria. Her attention was on the dark, distant ocean, with the pistol in her hand.

The tunnel was jagged and barely wide enough for a man to climb through. Jayse was glad for his glove and his suit, made thick for military use. Sharp rocks would have ripped him apart otherwise. Horizontal at first, the passage was filled with seawater, but it soon started to ascend, creating air pockets above their heads. As the angle became sharper, their gear became more of a burden with the water level dropping below half.

"Do you have any idea where this goes?" Jayse asked, no longer needing the throat mic as his head came above the surface.

"Up," Cathal said simply.

"But where does it end?"

"I've no idea," Cathal said, pausing at what seemed to be a dead end. He looked back at the other two, then pointed above. "I think we can leave the bottles here," he said.

Jayse moved next to him and turned his helmet light up. The tunnel became a shaft ascending into a dark distance. They all took their packs off, leaving them leaning against the wall, then Cathal led the way again, climbing hand over hand. The shaft was narrow enough that he could wedge his legs against the opposite wall.

Along the arduous climb, their uniforms gave way to the sharp edges. The military-grade material shredded. "Is this how most of your missions go?" he asked Cathal as he pulled himself up, worried the shaft was getting even tighter.

"What do you mean? We haven't been shot at once. I think it's going great." Cathal vanished above Jayse. When the prince joined him, he saw why. There was a ledge and a spot where the tunnel turned. Cathal dropped to his hands and knees to crawl.

Again, Jayse felt the urge to ask if his friend had any idea where they were, but he knew the answer. Only moments later, he heard Cathal yell back, "Hey, I found a wall."

In the light of their helmets, Jayse could barely see the spot in front of his friend where the tunnel stopped. Stones had been cut and set with seams running between them. Cathal took out another one of the chemical pouches. He used his knife again to spread it and to chip away the mortar as it dissolved. "This one is a bit thicker." He passed something back. "Help me with this," he said, pushing heavy rocks back toward Jayse.

"What's this?" Talbert asked as the stones came to him.

Jayse didn't sound impressed. "The wall Cathal found."

Up ahead, Cathal took out another pouch. Though he'd moved a good deal of material, there was still more ahead of him. The stones were larger, too big to fit back into the tunnel. He did his best to wedge the chemicals into the seams around the edges of the tunnel, softening it as best he could, but when he pushed at the heavy block, it didn't move at all.

There was just enough room for Cathal to turn around. He put his feet against the wall and kicked. Jayse was right behind him. "How's that going?" he asked as Cathal's kicks became manic.

Jayse couldn't see Cathal sneering at him. Then, with one last boot, the foundation stone gave, moving a little. "Not bad," Cathal said with satisfaction.

"You still have no idea where we are, though, right?" Jayse was trying to imagine what was on the other side. In his mind, he pictured armed guards all standing around a stone in a hallway, watching it slowly push out. They'd have their weapons drawn, pointed at whoever was dumb enough to come in this way.

"We're about to find out." Cathal went back to kicking. He hit it back and forth on either side, wiggling the stone.

"You know you're making a lot of noise?" Jayse asked.

Cathal stopped momentarily and took his pistol out, checking that it was loaded and ready to fire. "Whelp, I can't say I see another way, so. . ." He continued kicking. Finally, the stone fell completely out, leaving a small opening. It would be an incredibly tight squeeze.

Heat and light came through. It felt good after being in the cold water and in the tunnel, which wasn't much warmer. Then, past Cathal, Jayse saw the way the light danced. "Those look like flames," he said.

Cathal turned again and stuck his head in the opening. He said, "Yep, those are flames. Be careful getting out." Then he jammed himself into the hole. Talbert and Jayse watched him struggle. They heard him on the other side, making little noises of discomfort, "Yah! Ouch." His foot finally disappeared, and a moment later, they heard a hissing sound.

Jayse came forward and looked out. They'd managed to open a hole into a fireplace. There was a low flame burning in the hearth, with dried seaweed rolled into logs. Cathal had just poured out a bowl of water to dampen it, though the fire was too big to put out completely. It took up a quarter of the available space, which was big enough for five men to stand comfortably in. A rack for roasting meat was in the center and though they could smell that something had been recently cooked, the rack was empty.

Cathal reached back to help the others out and into a large dining hall, which was dark and luckily empty. His helmet was streaked with soot, though his light was still shining from it.

"Have you ever been here before?" Talbert asked while getting to his feet and looking around at the large empty room.

Jayse nodded. "I have, but not in years. It was a lot more crowded then. Where is everyone?"

Cathal leaned against a long table, one of many for the soldiers and nobles berthed here. He kept his voice low as he let his eyes slowly take in the space. "If I had to guess, I'd say on the way to Anchor Home, to join the search for your wife. Silly them." Cathal tilted his head.

Jayse looked at his friend. "You think she's here?"

"The only sub docked in the moon pool was a small special forces unit, smaller even than the one that attacked us. Just the kind I'd use for covert work like an abduction."

"And in so doing, create an excuse to make war on the True Grannusians," Jayse added. Not for the first time, he thought of how much this could cost his people. What a fine distraction it was.

Cathal nodded. "Or at least bully them."

"It won't go well. You must know that?" Talbert asked.

Before Jayse could answer, he heard a door swing open and voices approaching.

"Shut your lights off. Get back!" Cathal warned, pushing the others up against the wall, behind the fireplace. He ducked beneath the nearest table as two men dressed in simple white servants' clothing entered, pushing a cart in front of them. The door they'd come through led to a kitchen where the lights were brighter. Their glow carved like a blade across the floor. On the cart were several covered dishes, and the smell of fresh food wafted into the air as they passed.

The servants didn't notice the fire had gone down, or the men hiding in the shadows, watching them. They moved with hurried steps, passing out into the corridor.

"Come on," Cathal said, going after them.

Jayse sniffed, feeling his stomach grumble. "Someone is about to have a nice meal."

Cathal tiptoed to the door. "Probably your cousin. Maybe your wife too. I'd say it's well past time for a family reunion." His pistol in hand, he opened it a crack and looked out into a vast corridor. "It's clear," he said, stepping into the brighter lights. Seeing each other and how tattered their gear had become, Jayse whispered, "So much for our disguises."

Cathal shrugged, examined Talbert, and said, "Stay behind us if we run into anyone." He touched one of the rips that revealed the Naiad's grey skin before turning and creeping forward. He added over his shoulder to Jayse, "And you try working on being more positive."

Burying his annoyance, Jayse laughed to himself as he shook his head, realizing how much Cathal enjoyed being here. They were in jeopardy, and he loved it, thrived on it. 'Be more like Cathal,' he told himself. It was an old mantra he often said while they were training together. With a long sigh, he settled his nerves.

CHAPTER 14

Deep's Blade was a fortress built for armies, not for aesthetics. The trappings of royalty flags and decorations claimed from the sea hung in the corridors. Talbert reached up and touched the skull of a young sea dragon. He took his hand away, following Jayse and Cathal.

The three men couldn't hear the dinner cart move on oiled wheels, barely making a sound, but it was easy enough to follow the smell and the voices ahead. They reached a corner and peered around, piling together, all trying to look. Cathal pushed the others back to keep from being spotted.

Not far away, two guards stood outside a large, heavy door. The cart disappeared inside, and the guards returned to their boring watch, leaning back against the wall. They were deep inside a fortress meant to be impregnable, neither expecting trouble.

"How do we get past them?" Jayse asked.

"Trickery of course. Stay here," Cathal said. He was gone before they could ask what he meant.

He stepped out, leaving Talbert and Jayse behind, looking at each other, wondering what he was up to. Cathal's pistol was in its holster, and he was holding his arm as if it were hurt. "Hey, can you guys give me a hand? I had an accident in the sub bay. There's no one else in this damn place," he called to the guards.

The soldiers wore helmets, covering their faces and dry-land uniforms. Both turned and looked, while Cathal plopped against the wall. "I'm really messed up, guys. Get me to the medical unit. Please," he said desperately.

One started toward Cathal, while the other stayed behind. Cathal threw himself to the floor, falling like a ton of bricks. Letting out a groan as he went still. That finally got both men to come forward and check on him.

'Hell of a performance, he missed his calling,' Jayse thought as he pointed his pistol, ready to order the men to drop their weapons. Neither guard bothered to look around the corner as they hurried over to check on him. They didn't see Talbert close in from behind. Pushing past Jayse, the Naiad didn't make a sound as he fell on the guards like a force of nature. Jayse almost reached out to stop him, but instead he pointed the pistol away and watched in shock at the man's speed and strength.

A lifetime of swimming and living deep in the ocean, under increased pressure, meant Naiads were naturally stronger than most humans. Talbert grabbed the guards by their collars and pulled them back around the corner. He put each man in a headlock and squeezed around their throats, dragging them up the corridor, where no one would hear.

With a violent wrench of a single long arm, he snapped one man's neck. The other grabbed his belt, trying to fight his fate and battle free, but Talbert shoved him down hard to the floor, first with his arm, then with his foot. He lifted his leg once and brought it down on the man's spine, crushing his back. The guard stopped struggling.

Jayse stared, open-mouthed, as Cathal got up and hurried over. "That was brutal," he said, looking at the two bodies.

"You didn't have to—" Jayse started, but he stopped, watching Talbert take his helmet off and drop it to the floor.

His dark eyes burned with rage as he stared at the bodies. "Do you think these were the men who killed my son?"

Searching the distance, making sure no one was coming, Cathal said, "I doubt it. I think they were just guards."

"Common soldiers," Jayse added, trying to watch his tone.

Talbert squeezed his fists. "My son wasn't even a soldier, just a boy."

Jayse and Cathal's eyes met, both thinking the same thing; They'd been soldiers once too. They'd stood posts just like these two. "Understood." Cathal nodded. "Let's get these guys out of the hall before anyone notices." He bent down, picked up a body, and dragged him toward the nearest door.

Out of sight, Cathal started stripping the man of his uniform. "Same plan, new gear," he said to Jayse, who dragged the other one.

One after the other, they realized Talbert hadn't come with them. Bent over, Jayse pointed back. "I don't think we have time for that." He grabbed Cathal's shoulder, and they hurried around the corner.

"I thought the girl would be the tough one," Cathal said as they rushed down the hallway. They saw the Naiad about to kick the door in. Cathal hurried to him and grabbed his arm. He whispered, "Woah, big guy! Let's take a breath."

Talbert threw the arm off and pulled back, ready to go through, but then he noticed Jayse. The prince ignored the Naiad, going past him and leaning into the door. He pressed his ear against it and put his finger to his lips, shushing the other two like children. He showed no fear of Talbert as he listened, hearing the person he'd come for.

There were several voices inside, and as thick as the door was, he recognized his wife's above the others. "You would ruin my family," she said in desperation.

A few people laughed at her, but then someone answered above the others in a satisfied tone, "You don't even deny it. Imagine, imagine what your husband would say. Imagine the scandal." Jayse assumed this was his father's cousin, the Duke Takia, though he'd only met the man a few times.

"You bastard," Daoine snarled.

Another voice spoke. Jayse wasn't sure who it was, but he sounded familiar, an elite accent that made him think the speaker wasn't from this territory. The stranger said, "If it wasn't for the spy. Losing him was the only reason we moved ahead with all this. I mean, it was going to happen anyway. It's what the gods demand. Still, it's a shame, wasting an asset is never good. I blame Ascari."

"What spy?" Daoine demanded.

The duke spoke again, "Your doctor, of course. You really should pay your medical staff more. They hold so many secrets, and poverty makes them easy to influence. He reported every detail of your pregnancy to my allies and myself. That's how we learned your family's little secret."

Jayse felt Talbert press in behind him. He'd calmed down a bit or was at least willing to be patient.

"But why this? Why take me?" Daoine asked.

The stranger's voice explained, "Leverage, of course. We needed to keep you and your unborn child safe. Starting a war isn't easy. It would happen no matter what, trust me; the high chief wanted it as much as we do. He just needed to be nudged, is all. And we wanted to make certain he didn't do anything drastic."

Jayse's eyes met Cathal's, who had leaned into the door as well. Until then, they thought the high chief had been behind everything, but he was being manipulated too.

The scraping of a chair on the floor as it was pushed back echoed out, followed by the tap of footsteps. Jayse was about to pull back, then he realized it was Takia pacing as he spoke. "The volcanism project, my life's work, has been slowed at every step. The fish-heads haven't openly attacked us, but they don't have to, not when the ocean and everything in it is their weapon. Accidents happen. Creatures we've never seen before rise from the depths to harass us."

"You're risking everything. A peace that's lasted generations," Daoine said.

"I'm putting us in a war that was already happening. Your father is weak. He sits on a throne he doesn't deserve, while the Grannusian send dirty half breeds to spy on us, a people the gods say shouldn't exist," the duke insisted.

"My lord, I doubt that boy was a spy," a gruff voice said.

"Maybe not, but he still had his uses." Duke Takia agreed with a little laugh. Jayse and Cathal looked back at Talbert, wondering if he was assuming the same thing. He was. The Naiad's face darkened as he backed up and took a deep breath. Jayse and Cathal barely had time to move as he drove his foot forward.

The doors exploded in, nearly coming off the hinges. "Murders!" Talbert screamed.

Inside, two men sat at a long, elegantly set table with Jayse's wife in between. Plates and serving dishes loaded with an elaborate meal—breads and meat, fruits, and vegetables—were displayed before them. The duke was obviously showing off for Daoine, putting out a meal rarely seen in the north. He stood just behind her chair, leaning over. As Talbert burst in, he stood back and froze, rooted to the ground with shock.

The servants with their carts were on the opposite side of the room, in the middle of refilling one of the men's wineglasses. Further behind them, by another exit, were two armed guards. None reacted fast enough to stop the outraged Naiad.

Talbert came forward with all the strength and force of an ocean storm. He never reached for his flechette pistol. With it, he could've executed most in that room. Instead, he pulled a large, ceremonial knife, like his son's. The duke, Jayse's cousin, had the misfortune of being the first in his path.

Talbert roared, and Takia's eyes went wide as the blade came down, hacking like an axe into his shoulder where his neck attached. Talbert had such strength that the blade carved deep into the duke's chest. It passed through his fine clothing and jewelry, his veins and arteries, not stopping until it reached his still-beating heart.

Jayse looked into the room. His wife's eyes fell on him, but his helmet hid his face. The way she started to her feet made him wonder if she recognized him. More than likely, she was only backing away from the outraged Naiad.

When they kidnapped her, she'd been in her nightgown but now, she wore traditional Northern garb, tailored for her pregnancy. They were warm breeches and a robe-like top, trimmed in the fur of a beast that hunted the ice sheets. Jayse saw the man sitting next to her, and he put a face with the stranger's voice. He'd met him a few days before; this was Lord Beleeze, the Tamerlane envoy.

Beleeze hurried to his feet and grabbed Daoine's arm as he backed away. Her pregnant belly bounced against the table as he dragged her behind him. At first, it would be easy to think he was saving her from the outraged Naiad, but as he purposefully kept her between them, Jayse realized that wasn't his goal. He was intent on keeping her as a prisoner or as a shield if need be.

Talbert barely had time to dive beneath the table, knocking chairs out of his way as the guards put their rifles to their shoulders and fired. The duke's body hit the ground as the table and walls exploded with bullets ripping into the carefully prepared meal and the tastefully decorated room.

Using the doorway for cover, Cathal returned fire. The flechettes struck one of the guards in the chest, casting him back, but failing to pierce his armor with a killing blow. Jayse tried to fire at the other guard, but Beleeze and his wife crossed in front, ducking low, forcing the guard to hold his fire. Jayse watched them go out the far door, following the servants who'd already made their escape.

The last man at the table, Commander Skellis, wore no armor, but a dark, unmarked military uniform. He got up and grabbed cutlery from the table, a large carving knife meant for the meat. With practiced skill, he slung it at Talbert, whose head peeked out while the fire was interrupted. "Die, you monster!" he shouted as the knife lodged in Talbert's shoulder.

Skellis grabbed a second knife and leapt across the table, coming for the Naiad who murdered his lord. Talbert got his arm above his head before the second blade could drive into his neck. His knee on the ground, he tried to get up and defend himself.

"Sir, move!" one of the guards called, trying to get a bead on Talbert. Cathal took the moment to move across the floor. He stayed low, beneath the table, crawling like a bear, right over Duke Takia's body while Jayse fired from the doorway. The small darts went high, missing the soldiers but distracting them long enough for Cathal to close the distance. He came up with his dive knife in hand, shoving the short rifle to the side and burying the blade in the guard's armpit, finding soft flesh where there was no armor plating.

The guard tried pushing him away, but Cathal had the strength and training of a grappler. Tripping the man, he tossed the guard aside and kicked his rifle clear. The second guard turned to fire, but Cathal was too fast. Throwing all his weight into this second man, grabbing the rifle, he pulled it forward and performed a hip toss.

Jayse looked at his friend, then at Talbert, who'd gotten to his feet. He tried to choose which one needed his help more. Remembering how easily Talbert had killed two soldiers outside, and seeing he had only a single opponent, he ran to Cathal while his eyes stayed on the door his wife had been dragged through.

The first guard Cathal attacked was still on the floor, bleeding from his side and looking for his rifle. Jayse could've passed him by and been after Daoine, but he didn't know how long Cathal's furious attack would keep these two at bay, and he couldn't abandon his friend.

The closest guard found his weapon, but before his fingers could close on the grip, Jayse stepped on his hand. "Don't," he said, standing over the man, pointing the flechette pistol just below his helmet. The guard didn't listen. He reached for Jayse's hand, forcing the prince to pull the trigger. The little bards went through the man's palm and into the side of his neck, where the armor was thinnest. Ripping through the soft flesh of his throat, they buried themselves in the floor on the other side.

"Dammit!" Jayse watched the man try to cover the wound. Seeing him bleed out was a stomach-churning sight. The guard writhed and collapsed. Resisting the urge to throw the weapon away, Jayse cursed again, screaming at the dying man, "Why did you do that?" In his years of military service, in his entire life, he'd never been forced to take a human life.

Aside from his grandfather dying in a soft bed, before this adventure, he'd never seen anyone die, not like this, with violence upon violence. He looked at Cathal. His friend had ducked down behind the other guard. He had him in a rear chokehold, his thick arm just below the guard's helmet, squeezing tight. "Go." Cathal motioned with his head toward the door.

Jayse bit his lip and nodded, trying to shake off what he'd done, then he reminded himself why he was here. These people had taken his wife. 'They'd started this,' he thought, following Beleeze into a back hall.

CHAPTER 15

Moments before Talbert crashed through the door, Commander Skellis looked at his duke. He'd served Takia his entire adult life. He knew he was a man of vision, a true northerner like himself. People were different up here. They lived above the cold ocean, through long winters with creatures hunting the depths below them, creatures that the Grannusians claimed they didn't control. It meant that northern men, like Skellis and Takia, always needed to pay attention and think of survival. There was a saying, 'Even the thickest ice could give way.'

As the duke carried on, flaunting victory before Princess Daoine and the envoy from Uppsala, Skellis sipped his wine and let his guard slip, reveling in the joy of a job well done. In the south, the high chief was calling on all the tribes, calling on a council of war. They'd finally put those fish-heads in their place. In his lifetime, Skellis would see islands rise from the sea where real people could make their homes.

True, they'd be beholden to a distant emperor. For a man like Skellis, a low-born soldier, what difference did it make who he took his orders from, as long as they were human? Not some species made of worms and fish, some conglomeration so strange that it turned his stomach.

He thought of killing that Naiad boy, and his lip curled in a smile. The True Grannusians wanted them to abandon their humanity. That's what they wanted the humans of this world to become. At that moment, the doors burst open, sounding so much like the sudden cracking of ice. There stood one of those things. It was as if Skellis had conjured the creature with his thoughts.

The Naiad moved fast, so incredibly fast, attacking his duke. It wedged its knife into him, carving him like the meat on the table. The speed, the aggression, it made Skellis sit back in shock and fear, feelings he wasn't used to. He buried them as the sound of automatic weapons fire filled the room. The table and the wall exploded as the Naiad dropped away, finding cover. Skellis felt rage boil over at this thing for causing him to fear.

He took a knife from the table and threw it with practiced skill and with a better angle than the guards, managing to sink the blade into the Naiad's shoulder. He'd been aiming for its throat. 'That'd be next,' he thought as he grabbed a second blade and launched himself across the table.

He was aware that the shooting had stopped, but he wasn't sure why. He saw other men in the doorway, but his focus was only on the Naiad. The creature was getting back to his feet when Skellis jumped down on him with both his feet, driving it into the far wall. "Kill you," Skellis growled, bringing the knife down.

Talbert managed to get his arm up, blocking the blade. The Naiad reached for Skellis' throat, closing a single hand over the soldier's thick neck. Skellis may have been angry, but he was still trained for hand-to-hand combat. He wasn't surprised by the Naiad's strength. He smashed his open fist down on the knife in the creature's shoulder, pushing it deep, past his clavicle. Talbert's fingers loosened around his neck as his hand went numb with the nerves severed.

Behind them, Cathal choked out one guard, and Jayse had killed the other. As Cathal squeezed, he told the prince, "Go, go after your wife!"

Talbert nodded, glad that the young prince was going. He seemed to be a better surface dweller than most. With the knife still hooked over his arm, the Naiad used his incredible strength to twist and throw Skellis into the corner.

Talbert glanced briefly at Cathal getting to his feet, letting the unconscious guard drop to the floor. "Help your friend," he called after him, hearing the sound of more soldiers approaching. "I will hold them here." His dark eyes returned to Skellis, who stayed low, with his knife in his hand.

Cathal nodded, picking up a rifle from one of the fallen guards. He said, "You don't have to do this."

"Just go. This one is going to tell me who killed my son." Talbert's hand was on the flechette pistol, still in its holster.

"There's more coming," Cathal called as he backed out.

"Good," Talbert said. He kept his eyes on his opponent. He trusted his strength and the weapon in his hand against the unarmored man, but Skellis knew better. He was well within the Naiad's guard, he had a blade and knew the Naiad's anatomy.

"Your son? You mean that corpse we left in Anchor Home, he was your son?" Skellis asked, staying low.

"You're the one who killed him?" Talbert snarled.

Skellis tilted his head. "I captured him. Questioned him and put the gun in the hand of the man who did." As the pistol cleared Talbert's holster, Skellis feigned in one direction, then, quick as a striking snake, moved in the other. He closed the few steps to the Naiad as Talbert pulled the trigger.

The shot went wide over Skellis' shoulder as he drove his blade into the Naiad's side, slicing down on his gill plates. The vascular vessel carried oxygenated blood from the Naiad's gills. Talbert was using his lungs to breathe on the surface, but blood still filled those engineered organs, and now it was quickly draining out, having a similar effect as slicing a man's throat. It had happened so fast that Talbert didn't understand what was happening, why he was becoming so weak.

Skellis came up, locking onto the arm with the pistol, closing it under his armpit while stabbing again, driving the blade into Talbert. They were so close, it looked like they were embracing. Skellis saw the rage in Talbert's dark eyes quickly fade as the Naiad's body became heavy. "You should've stayed in the deep," he said, letting him fall. Behind him, he heard soldiers approaching.

He bent and picked the pistol up from the ground, then stuck his head back in the hall. "You men, follow me," he called to the three soldiers closing in.

CHAPTER 16

Coming out of the back entrance, Jayse found himself in a narrow hallway for servants to pass unnoticed. There were cleaning supplies, empty shelves for dirty dishes, and replacements if a plate or bowl needed to be exchanged. His last sight of the bullet-ridden table made him think they weren't nearly prepared enough.

There were only two directions Beleeze could've gone with his wife. Jayse tried to listen, but all he could hear inside the helmet was the beating of his own heart. He threw it to the floor as his wife's voice echoed around a corner, "Let me go!"

He heard a smack and felt his face flush with rage, picturing that Uppsalan lord striking his wife. With his pistol squeezed tight in his hand, he charged ahead. But when he came around the corner, he saw Lord Beleeze on the floor, his nose bleeding. Daoine stood with her fists closed and her round belly heaving with every angry breath, staring down at him. She turned toward her husband with her hands up, ready to fight.

"Jayse?" she asked as her eyes widened, seeing his face for the first time.

He had the pistol pointed at the ground, ready to come in and embrace her, but as he took a step forward, Daoine heard Beleeze get up. She leaned in, grabbed the weapon from her husband, and turned back, pointing it at the Envoy from Uppsala. Without hesitation, she pulled the trigger. The small flechettes ripped Beleeze's leg apart. "Stay," Daoine ordered him.

Jayse's eyes widened, shocked by her speed and viciousness. With the weapon still pointed at the man, she asked her husband, "What are you doing here?"

"It's good to see you too," Jayse said, not bothering to ask for the pistol back.

She rolled her eyes. Then, holding the weapon up, she pushed into him for a kiss. It was quick and deep. "Better?" she asked as their eyes met.

"Yes, better." He nodded, though he was still distracted by Beleeze, squalling in pain.

She smiled. "You smell like low tide, by the way." Then her expression quickly changed as someone came around the corner.

They both turned at the sound of Cathal hurrying behind them. He skidded to a stop, taking in the scene and seeing the pistol in Daoine's hand with the man on the floor, groaning in pain, gripping his leg. The weapon pointed to his chest as Cathal held his hands up, realizing she didn't know who he was.

Jayse put himself in front of his friend. "Don't shoot, it's Cathal."

Cathal's ruined uniform made him stand out from the other soldiers. "Yeah, please."

She shook her head. "I can't believe you two are here."

Cathal shrugged. "I had nothing else to do, and a guy's trip sounded fun."

She glanced past him. "It's just you two?"

Waving for them to follow him, Cathal started back to the dining room. "We have a big, angry Naiad with us too." He reached the door, making it as far as the threshold, before realizing it was no longer an option. Cathal saw Talbert lying across the table, not moving, while soldiers rushed into the room, following the last man who'd been sitting at the table.

Cathal almost stumbled backing out. "Yep, not going that way." He pointed up the hall, yelling, "Go, go!" He stopped for a second to close the door and drop a shelf in front of it. The extra plates and bowls crashed to the ground as it wedged between the walls.

Neither the prince nor the princess questioned him, turning and charging ahead. They jumped over Beleeze, who dragged himself and his destroyed leg to the wall. The sound of gunfire filled the hall as the soldiers found the door blocked.

Daoine was in the lead. "Do you know where you're going?" Jayse asked.

"No, but Beleeze was taking me somewhere, somewhere he thought he'd be safe." She came to a flight of stairs. They were narrow like the hallway, going up and down. She paused, looking in both directions, then she turned back as Cathal caught up. "What do you think?"

He shrugged, keeping the rifle and his eyes behind them. "Down, let's try down."

Daoine held the pistol out in front as she descended. The steps twisted in a tight circle, going further into the fortress. At the bottom, they came out in an industrial-looking passage with pipes running everywhere. "What about Talbert?" Jayse asked Cathal as they stepped away from the stairs.

"He's dead," Cathal said, glancing back up the steps. He heard heavy combat boots coming down.

Jayse shook his head, angry at the loss, counting the lives that'd already been taken and wondering how many more would be next if he didn't get his wife back to Anchor Home. She'd gotten ahead of him and found a heavy door, more like the hatch on a sub. Her ear against it, she listened before gripping the two handles and twisting until they released. She opened the door a crack and peeked out.

"What do you see?" Jayse asked.

Before she could answer, the small hallway was rocked by the sound of more gunfire. Cathal was on his knee, taking what cover he could at the bottom of the steps and firing up. "Go!" he yelled.

Daoine opened the door just enough for her and Jayse to slip through. They entered a massive room where the musty air was so full of salt water, it instantly made their skin feel wet. The ceiling was thirty meters overhead. Ramps and catwalks ran everywhere along the side and over a large pool. They'd seen this from below, along with the lone sub docked on the far wall.

Unfortunately, they also saw at least a dozen men, some soldiers, and some technicians, but all turned to see what was happening as Cathal jumped through the hatch with bullets ringing off it as he shut it behind him.

CHAPTER 17

Leaning against the heavy metal hatch, Cathal grabbed the handles and held them locked in place. As bullets struck it from the other side, blisters popped out in the metal, swelling like hives. He took the rifle that he'd grabbed upstairs and wedged the barrel under one latch and beneath the other, jamming it shut. It wouldn't last for long as somebody was already moving it behind the door, trying to knock the weapon out of place.

Noticing how engaged with the door his friend was, Jayse asked, "What are you doing? We've got company."

Cathal looked up, then he pointed back at his rifle. "Too much company and no bullets." He glanced at the men around the large moon pool.

A dozen men spread throughout the room. Most were technicians or custodians, cleaning and maintaining the docks that ran out into the pool. But there were also soldiers, a group of three and a group of two, who started over from two different directions to investigate. As Jayse searched for a way to escape, Cathal waved his arm at the soldiers. "Hey, hey, you guys over here! Over here! Give us a hand."

"What are you doing?" Jayse's eyes widened as he looked back at his friend.

Cathal ignored him, calling again, "We're under attack. They're trying to get in." He pointed to the hatch. He and Jayse were still wearing the uniforms from earlier, and Cathal had his helmet on.

He grabbed Daoine's arm and pulled her to him, leaning in, he said, "Hide that gun."

The princess did as he asked, putting the weapon in her waistband as the five soldiers closed in. "I need to get this prisoner on the sub," Cathal said in a commanding voice before pointing his thumb at the hatch. "Make sure these intruders don't get to her. I'm counting on you men." To demonstrate his point, a heavy banging at the door rang out as something large smashed into it again and again.

One of the men nodded as the others unshouldered their rifles and pulled handguns out. Another asked, "Who are they?" But Cathal was already moving away, holding tight to Daoine as if she were truly his captive.

"Hurry," Jayse said in a low, rushed voice as he led the way, speed walking along the pool. They made it ten of the fifty meters to the sub before they heard the sound of gunfire and the door being pried open. "Run!" Cathal said, pushing at Daoine's back as the three broke into a full charge, dashing by the water's edge.

At the hatch, the weapons fire stopped as quickly as it started, followed by raised voices. The loudest was Skellis giving orders to the soldiers and pushing his way past them. Cathal glanced over his shoulder, seeing men pointing their rifles in response to Skellis' commands.

The trio passed a pile of crates and was about to turn the corner, going around the edge of the moon pool. It was only a short distance to the sub's dock after that, but they'd be completely exposed along the far wall. Grabbing Daoine and Jayse by the arm, Cathal pulled them back, ducking behind the cargo as bullets flew toward them.

"I was really hoping we'd get further," Cathal shouted while covering his friends from flying debris as round after round smashed into the crates. He took out his pistol and looked at the weapon, shaking his head. Flechettes weren't all that effective at a distance, especially against men in armor.

He saw Daoine take hers out as well. He pointed to it, telling her, "Give me that." When she didn't at first, he explained, "If you get the chance to run, I'll cover you, but if you start shooting, they're going to shoot back."

The weapon fire paused, and Cathal stuck his head out of the tiny alley, gauging their path. Workers who hadn't responded at first were closing in from the opposite side, while Skellis' party, which had grown to seven, blocked their way back. Cathal saw the sub, so close, sitting at its dock. Its hatch was even open, but there was no way to get to it. Not while they were surrounded.

"There's nowhere to go; you're trapped," Skellis called.

"Okay, agreed," Cathal called back, his voice calm and sardonic. "What would you suggest?"

"That you surrender," Skellis snapped.

"What happens then? Make us an offer." Cathal looked at the pool, wondering if it was an option. Diving deep enough, he might be able to make it, but he was trained. Jayse and Daoine weren't. Even with him staying behind to cover them, with so many soldiers, they had little chance.

"'Make you an offer?'" Skellis' voice vibrated with rage. "Get out here, or we'll kill you all and send the princess' corpse back to the high chief."

Cathal was still looking at the water as if it were the answer. Then he saw something moving down below the surface. "Okay, so that's your opening bid. I can't say I like it, but we've got to start somewhere."

Skellis answered him by blasting the crates.

Jayse grabbed his wife and covered her as best he could from the flying wreckage. Calling to Cathal, he said, "Stop messing with him. There's no way out."

Cathal smiled at his friend and shrugged. "Have a little faith." He turned back as the gunfire stopped and saw shadows on the floor. Men were approaching. Pointing both pistols, he hit the first soldier to come around the corner, pelting him with tiny barbs and pushing him back. Jayse pulled the trigger again, aiming for the man's shoulder joint while pointing his other weapon at the man behind him.

He fired into the second man's helmet, trying to block his view. The barbs sank into his eyepiece, making his head look like a porcupine. Cathal kicked the first man, knocking them both back a few steps, but more were behind. Skellis' entire squad had formed up on either side of the crates, ready to charge in and crush him.

Cathal backed away, holding the pistols ready. He planted his feet, knowing there was a good chance they'd take him, not thinking at all about dying, but not ready to lose either. Then he heard the sound he was waiting for. Something massive emerged from the water behind the soldiers. It roared as it broke the surface. Then there was more noise. Splashing and screaming. The sound of men fleeing for their lives.

A soldier ran into the little crack between the crates, but he wasn't rushing Cathal; he was fleeing for his life, trying to escape the sea dragons emerging from the moon pool. Cathal kicked the man squarely in the chest, pushing him back out, where teeth closed on him and dragged him into the air. He screamed, and his feet kicked while his torso was enveloped in the dragon's mouth.

"Come on," Cathal said, grabbing Jayse's shoulder and pulling him and Daoine behind. They emerged from the alley into a scene of chaos. The three sea dragons moved in and out of the water, snatching men from the walkway. Bullets flew, but few found their mark with the creatures diving and leaping, traveling so fast as they threw bodies in every direction. Any soldier's discipline was lost at the notion of being eaten.

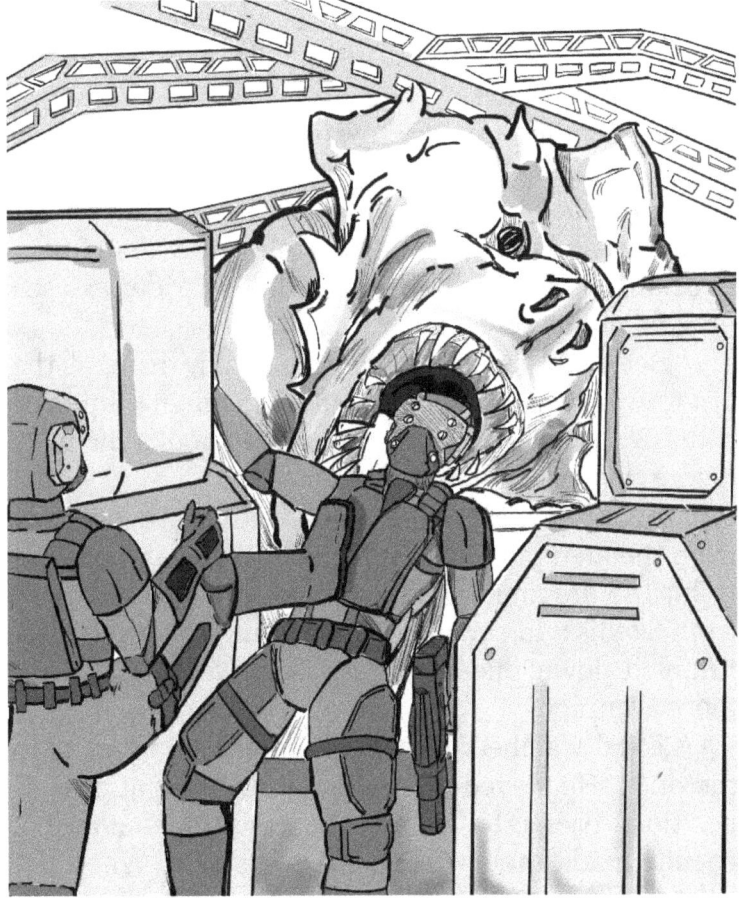

Just in front of Cathal, a soldier was pinned to the crates with a Naiad spear through his chest. Cathal took off his helmet, quite certain he didn't want to be mistaken for the enemy as he caught a quick view of Aysa riding her dragon and firing again. He saw Nasir here as well, on another mount, pointing a second spear gun.

"Let's go!" Cathal said, motioning for Jayse and Daoine to move. He handed the weapons to them. "Shoot anyone who gets in the way of you getting on that sub," he said, waving them along while he picked up the pinned soldier's rifle. He stayed back, watching them go, drawing a bead on Skellis' men who were firing at the dragons.

As Jayse led the way toward the sub, one worker tried to get in his way, swinging a wrench at his head. Though he had his pistol in hand, Jayse didn't bother shooting him. Rather, he barreled the man over, knocking him into the water, where a riderless sea dragon landed on him.

"Better to shoot him," Daoine said, firing at the other workers. Most were already giving up and running, trying to get out of the moon pool's chamber before they became lunch.

The water was getting cloudy with blood, not only from the men but also from the shots that'd managed to hit the dragons. The creatures were backing away from Skellis and two men who'd found cover behind a tumbled down pile of crates. They were firing with more accuracy.

Cathal watched Jayse and Daoine turn out onto the dock. He stayed on the far wall, firing at Skellis' position, trying to keep their heads down, as his friends made their way up the sub's side. When the rifle ran dry, Cathal threw it away and charged Skellis' position. Launching himself over the crate, he dove into the man's cover. Skellis saw it coming, and while he couldn't point his pistol in time, he managed to get his hands up and turn Cathal's momentum, throwing him out onto the walkway.

Cathal landed roughly, looking back to see Skellis close in on him, knife in hand. Cathal barely had time to get his arms up. The blade sank into his forearm.

"I know you," Skellis said in a growl. "You're that troublemaker."

"Yeah, I've got a reputation," Cathal said with a smile, though the pain in his arm was incredible. He drove his knee up into Skellis' groin. The commander groaned but didn't give up driving the blade forward. Cathal reached for his own dive knife, but Skellis pinned that arm down with his leg, kneeling on Cathal's fingers.

Ripping his blade back out, Skellis prepared to sink it into Cathal's chest. Cathal reached out, trying to grip his wrist, but his fingers wouldn't close, not with the nerves in his forearm severed. He looked at the blade coming down and had enough time to think, 'Anyone but this guy.' That's when water dripped down from behind Skellis. Cathal looked past him, feeling hot air on his face as a set of jaws closed, grabbing the commander. Cathal watched the teeth close, passing through Skellis' back and rib cage. To his credit, Skellis was still trying to stab Cathal even as the dragon dragged him away.

Past the horror, Aysa leaned out, staring over her dragon's head. Cathal pointed to the beast's mouth and shouted to her, "That's the one you wanted." The dragon's head went back, throwing Skellis into the air before opening its mouth to swallow him in a single bite.

Cathal looked at the other two soldiers behind their makeshift cover. "I'd give up if I were you guys." Their rifles couldn't have hit the ground faster.

CHAPTER 18

Immediately after climbing into the sub, Jayse went to the controls to initiate the engines and realized military vehicles differed greatly from civilian models. He may have served in the defense force, but he'd never piloted a combat sub built for special forces. "Any idea?" he asked Daoine, who was holding the pistol again, covering the hatch. The sounds of gunfire, men screaming, and the roaring of sea dragons had quieted down.

She glanced back, but a familiar voice called her attention to the hatch, "Hey guys, everything is fine out here. You can come up."

Jayse went first, going up the ladder and sticking his head out. Cathal was below, holding a rag over his bleeding arm. He added, "Do you think you could find me a first aid kit? That guy got me pretty good." His voice was nonchalant, not bothered by the injury or the creature rising from the surface behind him.

Jayse's gaze locked on the sea dragon towering above the dock where it treaded water at eye level with the prince. He couldn't help noticing the blood on its teeth as its cold stare held him.

Aysa climbed down from the creature's back, stepping behind Cathal, making Jayse want to ask his friend, 'Did you ride on that?' But he couldn't find the words, feeling entranced. Two other dragons were further down the dock where Aysa's father, Nasir, climbed off his mount.

"Jayse," Cathal called his name, finally getting him to look down, "How bout' that med kit? And could you ask your wife to join us? She might like to meet the people who saved her?"

Jayse didn't have to go far to find the medical supplies. There was a pack stored just past the hatch. He held it up, and Cathal motioned for him to throw it. He tossed the red box while searching the chamber for reinforcements. "You think it's safe? We don't have to worry?"

Cathal had a rifle slung over his shoulder. He studied each entrance and shrugged. "I doubt it. If anyone were coming, they'd be here already. I think most of the troops are on their way to Anchor Home. The only people left are servants, and the prospect of being eaten will keep even the bravest back, especially when their lord has already been killed. But like I said, have Daoine come down and meet our friends." Cathal was opening the kit and starting to walk down the dock.

"Where are you going?" Jayse called, stepping further down the sub's side, reaching back to help Daoine through the hatch next.

"We left Lord Beleeze bleeding in that hallway. I'd like to ask him a few questions, find out why he was here."

Daoine had to be careful getting out. Her stomach was so large with the child inside. She said to Cathal, "He was trying to soften Tamerlane's next target. By sending us after the True Grannusians, we'd be left weak and ready for invasion. That's why I was taken, to force my father's hand."

Cathal returned and helped her off the ladder and onto the dock. She cleared her throat and turned to Nasir, whose arm rested on Aysa's shoulder after hugging her, glad that she'd survived the battle without injury.

There was a little blood on Aysa's grey cheek, as she asked Cathal, "That last man we killed, who was he?"

Cathal explained, "He was Duke Takia's right hand, his head of security, and the only one he'd trust to pull off this kidnapping, which led to the murder of your friend."

"And what of Talbert?" Nasir asked.

Cathal lowered his head, looking at the water. "He died bravely after killing the duke, the man who set this plan in motion."

Into the silence that followed, Daoine said, "The only one left from the conspiracy is Beleeze. Even if we brought him back, I doubt he'd say much." She looked at Nasir and Aysa, suggestively.

If Cathal understood what the princess was hinting at, he wouldn't let on, as he said, "I still think I should talk to him. I can be pretty persuasive."

Daoine shook her head and said through a tight jaw with her fists closed, "We don't have time, not when we have a war to prevent. I need to get home. It's the only way to stop my father." She motioned to the sub. "Now, please, can you get this damn thing moving?"

Cathal looked ready to argue. His feet were locked to the ground, but Jayse grabbed his arm and said in a low voice, nodding to the Naiads, "I think she wants a moment." Daoine had moved closer to the father and daughter.

Cathal's shoulders were locked, but he agreed. "Thank you for your help," he said to Nasir and Aysa. "If you ever need a friend on the surface, call on me." Nasir nodded to him, and Cathal turned, disappearing through the hatch. Before Jayse could follow, he glanced back at his wife. She leaned into the two

Naiads, her hand on her belly as she urgently whispered to them. Her face was pulled tight, and her lips moved in a hurry.

The Naiads stood back. Jayse watched Nasir reach forward and laid his hand on Daoine while Aysa's dark eyes widened, staring at the princess with her mouth open. Daoine's face was damp when she turned to climb back up the sub's side, but before she could leave, Nasir took her arm and pulled her back to him. He reached past the round belly and hugged the princess. Jayse saw the man's mouth move and heard the words, "It will be all right. When the time comes, we will help you."

Then, as the princess left them, father and daughter made their way down the dock. Jayse helped Daoine to the hatch, seeing that her tears were now dry. He wanted to ask her what the matter was, but he knew his wife, if there was something she wanted to tell him, she would in her time. Questioning her would get him nowhere.

He took one last look at the Naiads, who were going toward one of the doors into the fortress. Jayse asked, "Where are they going?"

"I think they plan on taking care of Beleeze," Daoine said simply.

"'Take care of?' What does that mean?" Jayse asked, though he knew the answer.

Daoine's face was dark. "As long as he's never seen again, it doesn't matter what it means." That darkness reminded him so much of Daoine's father. It left him unsettled, especially knowing that facing the man was their next task.

CHAPTER 19

Passing through the northern ocean and into the south, the attack sub was swift and well handled by Cathal, who had been trained as a pilot for several types of craft. Though it had room for a small party of men, the sub felt tight to Jayse, whose wife had mostly been silent since they left Blades Deep.

Cathal told her the story of their adventure, alluding to their near-death experiences with humorous disregard. Daoine didn't find it funny. Distracted by worry, she wondered what her father would do to Cathal and Jayse when they got back. "He's not the one who planted the tracker on me. Who tried to kill me," Jayse said, thinking of the attack sub that fired on them near Twilight.

She shook her head. "It doesn't matter. We have a story he may or may not believe and little evidence to support it."

"We have you. You're his daughter." Jayse said. He'd always known the high chief could be difficult, but he'd shown he loved Daoine often enough, giving what little warmth he was capable of to her and Cormack.

"I am. But..." She closed her fists in frustration as her brows tightened, holding back tears. "Things change. I know you don't get this, that you can't imagine it, but you can't always count on the love of a parent." Claiming she was exhausted, she went to the back of the sub and spent much of the trip lying across the crew bench, staring at the ceiling. Something more than her father bothered her, but Jayse knew she'd volunteer nothing, not until she was ready.

As they approached Anchor Home, Daoine asked for the comms unit and for privacy. Jayse went forward to Cathal, closing the hatch to the crew compartment behind him. It wasn't long before she tapped on the metal, asking him to open it again. "I've made arrangements for you two when we get home. You'll wait in a safe house while I go talk to the high chief."

"You think that's necessary?" Jayse asked.

"He's about to go to war with the True Grannusians. You went to their city and helped the Naiads he believed kidnapped me. The people behind this may have wanted to force him into action, but don't think for a moment this wasn't something my father wanted." She stared out into the water. "I have no idea what he'll do now. If he'll even listen. But I want you safe."

Jayse noticed the way her hands cradled her belly, supporting its weight. He reached out and touched her. "It'll be all right."

"I hope so," she said.

A few kilometers out from Anchor Home, the monitors came alive with sonar contacts. The island was surrounded by ships, massive submarines, aircraft carriers, and nimble skimmers that made up the backbone of the Grannus defense forces, serving as troop transports and quick response vehicles. There were hundreds of attack subs, many larger than the one they were in. Cathal slipped through them, giving the most current military clearances, making his way toward the palace. It wasn't until they were well within the perimeter that he diverted, going to a civilian wharf where fishing boats pulled up with the day's catch. He passed by, running silent and scraping the mucky bottom before pulling into a warehouse, passing below a rolling door that stopped at the water's surface. Inside, Cathal brought them higher, rising from the water.

A lone figure stood by the edge of the small pool. Light came through opaque windows along the block walls. Jayse went first, climbing out, insisting he wanted to make sure it was safe. Through dusky, pale lighting, his eyes locked on someone he wasn't expecting to see.

Ascari, the commander of Grannus' defense force, bowed. "My prince, I'm glad to see you returned in one piece."

"Commander Ascari?" He looked around the warehouse, checking to make certain there weren't soldiers in waiting, ready to arrest him.

"Don't worry, I'm the only one here. I'm glad your mission was successful."

Before Jayse could open his mouth to ask how he knew, Ascari explained, "Daoine radioed me. You may struggle with the notion, but she trusts me. Perhaps I can earn yours as well."

Jayse touched the cold, wet sides of the sub, glancing back at his wife below him. "Trust goes both ways. And I get the feeling there are things I haven't been told."

"There are," Ascari agreed before changing the subject and pointing toward the door. "The safe house is just a few meters away. Though you may certainly stay in this lovely place until we settle things. As long as you remain out of sight. I don't think it should take long to see which way our high chief leans."

"So, no answers," Jayse asked.

Ascari went closer to the water's edge on the rickety old landing. "I serve the people, not the throne. We must stop this war before it starts." He glanced at the ceiling. "And I believe you know as well as I, we have other things to worry about."

'The Uppsalan fleet,' Jayse thought. They made eye contact, and each knew the other understood. He finished climbing out and reached back to help his wife. She struggled out of the hatch, leaving Jayse to wonder if this adventure had any effect on the child inside her.

He thought back to three days before, when they were meant to meet her doctor, a man who supposedly drowned. Something was bothering him, itching at the back of his mind as he remembered his cousin bragging at Blades Deep. He and Ascari helped Daoine across to the dock. After she settled on solid ground, he touched her belly. "Perhaps, you should see a doctor, make sure everything is okay?"

"Later, there will be time later," she said, brushing his hand away, then reaching up to touch his face. "First, let's do everything we can to get back to our son."

Jayse felt guilt wash over him like ice water. He'd been gone so long. He worried about what it had done to the boy.

Cathal exited next and looked less surprised. "Commander." He nodded to Ascari, congenial as ever.

"Captain," Ascari returned the acknowledgment with something bordering on warmth.

Jayse had an eyebrow raised as he stared at Cathal, who shrugged. "So, maybe I'm not completely unemployed."

Ascari explained, "Captain Cathal is far too resourceful to let go completely. He's what you might call a free agent. A bit too much of a free thinker at times too, but we still talk, and he's willing to help out as long as it doesn't compromise his principles."

"Playing all sides," Jayse asked, looking at his friend.

Cathal jumped across to the dock. The smile went away from his face as he shook his head. "No, not playing. Talking sometimes is a problem for you noble born. Killing is much easier. I try to keep you all from defaulting to it."

"Speaking of which, if you would join me, Princess?" Ascari motioned to the door. Daoine hugged her husband, promising to see him again, then she went with the commander. Before exiting, he disguised her in a simple robe with the hood drawn up. Given that most people on Anchor Home wore clothing fitted for the tropical climate, it wouldn't be the best camouflage, but they had little choice hiding a very pregnant princess.

Cathal and Jayse heard the sound of a skimmer lifting off from the ground. Its heavy turbines shot out over the water and faded into the distance. "Now what?" Jayse asked, trying to look out through the dirty glass.

"Now we wait and hope the high chief is less of a cantankerous turd than I think," Cathal said.

"I wouldn't get my hopes up," Jayse warned, still looking.

Cathal gave him time with his thoughts, then the sunlight began to fade. It was barely past midday. Cathal suggested, "Maybe we should wait in the sub, in case we have to get out of here."

Jayse turned to the black object that the sub had become. "There'd be no point. I'm not going anywhere without my son and wife."

As a moon circling a distant gas giant, the days moved strangely on Grannus. Every few rotations, there was a false night as they passed behind Altor, traveling in the giant's shadow. These eclipses carried with them superstitions, some traced back to legends before humans made their way to this water world, when the only known colonies were on Tairnish, a world far closer to the giant. Ancient stories say that humanity first arrived in this star system as refugees, children with a lost history.

Everyone knew what caused the lights to vanish, but that did nothing to offset the racial dread when Altor claimed the sky. True night would follow hours from now as this part of Grannus rotated away from the twin suns that gave this world life.

He heard Cathal, who shuffled about, stop and rub his hands together in the dark. "Another jail break. I'm game." Then his friend found a lantern and sparked it to life. He flipped over a couple of ancient, dust-covered chairs and sat, motioning to the opposite one. "Trust me, the safe house isn't much nicer, anyway."

"You've been there?" Jayse asked, and Cathal smiled before he passed time by telling his friend about his other adventures.

When the light from the twin suns returned, it was brief and pale, fading into true night. They heard the sound of the door unlocking. Ascari came back in. "Gentlemen, it's done. I believe you're safe to return home. Princess Daoine will meet you there."

"I'm sure he was happy to see his daughter," Cathal said.

Ascari nodded. "Yes, I suppose."

"He didn't listen to her? Did he?" Jayse asked.

Ascari shook his head and crossed his arms. "I'm not sure. I don't believe he liked what he heard. I don't know what he's going to do." He motioned out to the water. "In his time as high chief, he's never had such a force gathered. Every chief and lord came to aid him. There have been conflicts over the volcanism project. Delays brought on by attacks on the drill crews. Creatures we've never seen before rising from the deep. The True Grannusians deny any purposeful action, but the high chief doesn't believe them. He may still be looking for a way to apply pressure."

"That would be a mistake," Cathal said.

Ascari tilted his head, and his lip twisted. "As I said, we'll have to wait to see what he does. But for now, let's get this man back to his family."

Ascari brought the two outside. The docks were empty and quiet, with most returning to their tightly built dwellings further inland. Anchor Home rose on rolling hills, with apartment upon apartment, built of white block that seemed to shine in the starlight. Jayse saw Tairnish tracing across the sky, burning red in the radiation of nearby Altor. Directly above them was the dark spot where the Star Blossom blocked all light. It was a gift the Grannusians shared freely, letting the people of this world get to the ships they used for trade and defense. One more reason not to anger their neighbors.

They stepped into Ascari's skimmer and took off, blazing across the water, just above its surface, then coming down a few miles away at one of the palace's docks. There was little room with so many warships tied up. As they passed a guard post, Jayse heard voices everywhere. All about were nobles and their men, there at the high chief's request.

Many of them looked at Jayse questioningly, but he kept his eyes down and followed Ascari, whose pace didn't invite anyone to stop him. Close to his quarters were far fewer foreigners and more guards loyal to the commander. It wasn't until then that Ascari said, "The high chief has not made any announcement about Daoine yet. To be honest, he seemed to be in shock when he saw her, even more so when he heard it was you who brought her home."

Ascari held his hands up as he continued, "Daoine and her father were in private conference for a while. She said he plans to address the gathered clans in the morning about her return."

Finally, they reached the door to Jayse's apartment. One of the two guards outside swung it open for him. Cathal touched his shoulder before he passed inside and said, "I'm going to leave you here."

Turning around, Jayse stared at his friend with his unruly beard, teeth that were far from straight, and scars, each with a story behind them. Cathal's eyes were alight as always as he pointed inside. "Get in there, man; you earned this, you did this."

"Not without you. I would've been lost if it weren't for you." Jayse came in and hugged him.

Cathal squeezed and clapped him on the back as they came apart. He said, "Remember, families above and below us feel the way you do right now about the people they love. You're a good man, Jayse. That's why you're my friend."

The door closed, and Daoine came out to meet him. He hugged her past her belly. "He's already in bed, but there's little chance he's sleeping," she said. Jayse nodded and went past her to his son's room. The boy rushed to his father. Holding Cormack, Jayse said with tears in his eyes, "I'm so sorry I was gone so long. I'm so sorry."

The boy's voice was muffled. "It's okay, Daddy. I knew you were bringing Mommy back. I knew it, despite what Grandpa said."

Jayse felt a hot flash of anger, wondering what the high chief had told his son. He looked at his wife, and she shook her head, warning him not to ask.

They let Cormack stay up a while later, eating a frozen treat in their small kitchen. Then Daoine came into the boy's room and sat in a chair while Jayse read him a story. They went to bed together in the same room she'd been taken from. Neither could sleep.

Jayse asked her about her father's response, but she was vague with her answers. He got the sense it hadn't gone well, that no matter what happened, the man would insist on war or at least try to bully the true Grannusians. He knew it was time to act.

CHAPTER 20

Early in the morning, after a restless sleep, Jayse got out of bed. He looked at his wife, knowing her night had been troubled as well. He vaguely remembered rubbing her back in the dark until she finally settled.

Sneaking into his dressing room, he put on his finest royal garb and made his way to the chambers set aside for his father and his clan. His father and brothers greeted him warmly, all of them wanting to know where he'd been. He told the tale as they ate breakfast together. There were questions and ribbing at first, but as Jayse went on, they listened in rapt attention, shocked by the betrayal of Duke Takia, their cousin.

Agreeing to support Jayse, his father offered to go with him to the high chief, but Jayse remembered before this, when he'd tried asserting himself to his father-in-law and faltered. Whatever happened, he'd face the man down on his own. He left his father's chambers with a signed decree in hand, giving him power to speak for their people, and made his way to the heart of the palace.

Already, people were waking. The kitchens were hard at work, keeping up with the demands of all the guests. There were voices everywhere and watchful eyes. Many fell on Jayse as he made his way to the royal chambers. The guards stood and saluted him, and the high chief's royal attendant came forward.

"I wish an audience," Jayse demanded.

The thin attendant had surprisingly pale skin, as if he were kept from the light to match the white walls of the palace. He didn't even pretend respect as he sneered, "I'm afraid the high chief has yet to rise from his bed chamber."

Jayse glanced at a skylight and said in a voice loud enough for anyone passing to hear, "The suns have risen, and there is work to be done. I've come representing the northern tribes. Wake the chief." He held the decree up. The attendant read it but didn't react until Jayse grabbed his neck and pulled him forward, where in a lower but sharper tone, he said, "He will see me, or he will see our forces return to our territory. I'm here early to avoid embarrassing him in front of all these gathered tribes before he does anything stupid in an open forum."

The two guards didn't know what to do, having never seen the prince so angry, but knowing that to act against one such as him, could mean trouble. They stepped forward with shock lances in their hands. The attendant's eyes nearly bugged out of his head as he moved back. He glanced at the large doors to the royal chamber, carved from true wood imported from Uppsala.

He straightened his clothing and tried to cross his arms and deny Jayse again, but the prince stepped forward and pointed, "Do it."

The guards moved closer. One opened his mouth to speak, but then another person joined them, pushing through the crowd of onlookers who'd gathered. "Allow the prince to pass," Ascari said. The guards came to attention, their eyes wide. The attendant stared at the head of the Grannus defense forces, then nearly tripped over his own feet reaching for the iron door handle. Before he could pull it open, the decision was taken from him.

From the other side, there was a scream. A woman's voice echoed out, "Help, help!" The attendant pulled the door open, and the young Queen Talis ran out, still in her night clothes. This was the high chief's second wife, who he married after Daoine's mother passed away from an aneurysm. "Something's wrong with the high chief! He can't move," she cried as she nearly fell into Jayse.

Jayse, the attendant, Ascari, and two guards rushed through the door and back into the suite to the high chief's bed chamber. They found him in bed with his eyes bulging, filled with panic. His breathing was rushed, and his hands gripped the sheets. "Send for a doctor," Jayse yelled behind him as he touched his father-in-law. The man's eyes looked at him with something like recognition, but he couldn't move, and the sounds he made were unintelligible, rasping and grunting.

The doctor came with nurses and all the medical equipment they could carry, pushing past Jayse and the others. "He's having a stroke," he overheard the young woman say. "He needs surgery."

On this world, advances in medicine had been slowed by humanity's dependence on Grannusian healers. They needed aid from their neighbors for most internal injuries. There were human surgeons, but they were skilled only in delaying further injury until more advanced aid could be found. The medical staff unfolded a cot and loaded the high chief. Then the guards were tasked with carrying him through the winding halls back to the medical unit while word was sent out to find a healer.

True Grannusians could perform miracles. Their knowledge of medicine and biology wasn't only a field of study but the basis for all their technology. Their talents had led to a sort of laziness, an overreliance of the humans of Grannus on their arts, while places like

Uppsala and Tairnish had real surgeons, practiced in the necessary skills to remove a blockage from someone's brain. There had been few eras in humanity's history on Grannus, where there was more strife between the surface world and those below, which meant it was hours before a healer was found for the chief. All that time, the blood vessel in his brain remained blocked.

The healer arrived, covered in a robe, with the sound of her harness moving underneath. The bottles of water clinked, as glass and metal tapped into each other. True Grannusians weren't really female or male, but some took on the affect of sex when dealing with humanity. The healer did her best to remove the clot, but already, so much damage had been done. Placed in a medically induced coma, the high chief's breathing was artificially maintained through the night, but somewhere before the next dawn, his heart stopped beating.

Ascari delivered the word. He came to their chambers and told Daoine. He kneeled with his eyes on the floor as he said, "My queen, your father has passed away."

Daoine touched his shoulder, telling him to rise. "Thank you, Commander." Then she turned back to her husband, her hand supporting her belly that was so swollen, it looked ready to burst. Both were in shock, neither believing it could be their time. That they were now the rulers of humanity on this world.

Of course, there was more that had to be done before Daoine could start her reign. The clans needed to be consulted, and her claim examined, but with most of the chiefs already gathered, the process would be quick.

Before her second child was born, Daoine was given the throne. In her first few days, she stamped out the fires that would lead to war against the true Grannusians and welcomed their ambassadors back into the palace. Among them was the healer who would oversee her daughter's delivery.

Word of the Tamerlane fleet was spread amongst the people. They made ready for a war as the drive trails of the Uppsalan ships filled the night sky. The armada passed by, dropping into the belt around Altor, where they went about exterminating a people. The gods stayed silent as the queen finally told her husband the secret that had brought her to Blades deep as she tried to prepare him for what they would have to do.

Daoine had no doubt war would be visited on her people as well. She had to do everything in her power to maintain her authority and prepare the people of Grannus. There could be no doubt of her right to rule. Jayse knew this, and he hated it.

Epilogue

The capital was alive, waiting for the birth of the next Sidhe. They'd watched their queen's belly grow until every servant and soldier, every peddler in the street, waited for word that the child had finally arrived, believing it to be a happy occasion, a day where there would be feasting and joy.

A storm washed over Anchor Home that night when the birth pains came. Jayse and Daoine were in the royal chambers. The attendant ran in, hearing her scream with pain. These were the very chambers where Jayse had found her father. Daoine had the bed replaced, but the room was the same.

The Grannusian healer wasn't far. She entered, dressed in her robe, and sent the attendant away. The maids and servants, everyone near the royal chamber, were dismissed. A nanny was told to take Cormack somewhere far from the royal couple, to give them privacy, so the boy wouldn't have to hear his mother in pain.

After hours of labor, near the dawn, Daoine gave birth to a girl who they named Naiathne. The queen looked at her baby, seeing how strange it was, seeing its dark eyes and grey skin, believing at last a truth she'd been told by a cruel man.

Here was the leverage they'd held over her father, the high chief. This was why she'd been taken. Daoine's doctor had been an agent of Uppsala. For months, he'd hidden the truth, that through a genetic fluke, a Naiad would be born into their bloodline. It was proof that the Sidhe, the ruling family, highest of all the clans, wasn't as pure as they claimed.

Somewhere in their past were the genetic alterations that let people live below the sea.

Jayse sat on the bed next to his wife and held his daughter. The child had been dried off, but her skin still felt damp as tears rolled down from his eyes. Daoine tried to stay next to him, tried to look at the child, but it was too painful. Slowly, she inched away, moving to the edge of the mattress, as the Grannusian tended to her, cleaning and clearing the remains of the birth.

"When you're strong enough, they're waiting," the Grannusian said as she pulled the queen's nightgown down.

Daoine finally looked at her husband and her daughter. She knew he'd never forgive her for this. He'd never be able to move on, but it had to be done. They had to be strong. It was a single life against the freedom of their world. The queen got to her feet, staggering a bit with exhaustion. Ascari was waiting outside the door. "This way, my queen."

"Jayse, it's time," she said over her shoulder, not turning to look. Ascari took her arm and guided her back into a secret passage, one that led to the lagoon. Behind her, Jayse got to his feet, holding the girl. He kept his eyes low as he followed.

Out in the lagoon, Aysa and Nasir waited. The queen led the way, and the chief followed with the child. For a moment, Jayse wondered if the dragons were nearby. If his daughter would learn to ride one. It almost made him smile, a brief respite from his broken heart as he kissed his daughter on her forehead and put her in Aysa's arms. He and Daoine were silent as they watched the two disappear beneath the water and go out through the gate.

Rulers from across Grannus would send their condolences, believing the child died at birth. Rumors would circle, and eventually, the truth would come out. By then, war was no longer a foreign thought to the public; it was an undeniable fact.

When the story was finally told, as the Tamerlane armada surrounded their world, most could only reflect on Daoine's strength. The people loved their queen so much. they would follow her without question. They knew she would sacrifice everything to protect her people.

Pete A O'Donnell is the creator of

 Illadvisedstories.com, a children's story podcast where kids can listen to free and funny tales. He's a firefighter and EMT in his day job and has written and illustrated a picture book called the Merlin's Visit the Fire Station about his career. He holds a degree in journalism and creative writing from Queens University. His first book, The Curse of Purgatory Cove won the Royal Dragonfly award for best new author.

The Foreign Deep takes place a short time before the events of Book 2 of in The Giant's Shadow The Ocean Beyond. You can download a free character guide at his website PeteAODonnell.com